Brown

A NOVEL BY JAMES POLSTER

PUBLISHED BY

Text copyright ©2010 James Polster
All rights reserved
Printed in the United States of America

Published by AmazonEncore
P.O. Box 400818
Las Vegas, NV 89140

ISBN-13: 9781935597520
ISBN-10: 1935597523

To Nick Polster, the greatest guy of all time

ACKNOWLEDGMENTS

This novel won some awards, and the author gratefully acknowledges the support of the MacDowell Colony of Peterborough, New Hampshire; the Wurlitzer Foundation of Taos, New Mexico; and the Marin, California, Arts Council.

"You are the only man I know well who seems like myself to be aware of being on a pilgrimage."

— G. L. Dickenson to Bertrand Russell

ONE

I was in California. I'd been in Boston, working as a newspaper columnist, sports. My job was to cover anything that wasn't baseball, football, or basketball.

In the winter I'd drive up to Lake Placid and drink with the bobsledders; in the summer I'd roam New England and drink with the hydroplane racers.

All this drinking eventually led me into a rather free-wheeling brand of participatory journalism, and I began to cut out a perilous, yet unique little niche for myself. I raced, rowed, hunted, fished, pole-vaulted, windsurfed, skydived, cliff dived, was aced by Jimmy Connors, hustled by Minnesota Fats, and had my nose broken by the Montreal Canadians. As the only Harvard dropout on the staff, I was indulged by the editors whose fully realized Ivy League ambitions were securely framed and centered above their desks.

We are none of us, however, without enemies, even though the enemy may come from within.

In any case, I found myself ringside one night, Madison Square Garden, Wrestlefest '93, wondering, as emerging dean of participatory sports journalists, whether it would really become necessary to challenge the Human Hellhound.

Clearly, what was needed at this time was a sympathetic party with whom to discuss the matter. In short, someone to talk me out of it. My plan was to protest, then reluctantly retreat with honor and a week's worth of columns.

What was needed was someone reliable. Instead, I called my old girlfriend.

When we decided to get married over an emotional lunch of seaweed noodles at Mr. Chow's, the problem was where to live. Since ours was to be a modern marriage, there would be no question of one partner sacrificing, tipping the scales toward inequality. She hated Boston, and I had the usual qualms about Manhattan.

Resigned to resigning my position at the paper and relinquishing my rent-controlled apartment, I eventually agreed to San Francisco. New Orleans had been my first choice, but in the spirit of compromise, San Francisco won out as the city of highest mutually correlated approval.

We had, neither of us, any prospects or contacts in that direction. Just a couple of old friends and the memory of a romantic weekend a decade before. But this was now love, and this was adventure.

I bought new tires for the Austin Healey, picked up my fiancée outside Kaye's coffee shop on Lexington Avenue, and headed West.

By the approach into Winnemucca it had become obvious to all concerned that an egregious mistake had been made. I left her at the Trailways bus station with a Monte Christo sandwich, a Diet Pepsi, and four five-hundred-dollar traveler's checks.

So, I went on, San Francisco. Returning East was out of the question. I'd been given two elaborate going-away parties, and Rebecca Siegelman, the sports department's to-ken female, had been given the participatory beat. To me, the appointment of five-foot-two, one-hundred-fifty-eight-pound Rebecca smacked of sadistic overtones. Though this was mirthfully denied by the editors, my old job was none-theless quite filled.

Moreover, the Austin Healey was in no shape for a return run across the country. As the strongest remaining link to my former life, the car represented a certain emotional invest-ment, and I was somewhat reluctant to sell it. This reluctance was compounded by the realization that twenty years of Mas-sachusetts rust is not an attractive option in California.

There I was, a small apartment in North Beach, a dwindling bank account, respectful receptions at the daily papers (but ones which bore no fruit), and an aging English sports car.

TWO

I called Fillmore.

Fillmore was not a Harvard dropout. He had, in fact, parlayed his eastern PhD into simultaneous appointments at both Berkeley and Stanford. It had taken me a few weeks to get around to making this particular phone call because I knew that Fillmore, like most accomplished clinical psychologists, was completely insane.

"Hello, Fillmore? McGee Brown."

"Brown! All right, baby. Hey, great to hear from you. All right."

"Fillmore?"

"Yeah. What's shakin? Where are you, man?"

"San Francisco."

"Hey, me too."

As luck would have it, Fillmore was moonlighting as a bartender, working late shifts at Enrico's, three blocks away.

THREE

I entered the bar quietly. I hadn't seen Fillmore in three years, and there was no telling how advanced his overall state of deterioration had become.

He was, as expected, behind the bar making what might have been a Ramos gin fizz. It seemed that he hadn't changed his clothes since psychologizing that afternoon. He had on a very professional three-piece suit, but as a concession to bohemia, wore a distended Harley-Davidson T-shirt over his vest and tie, but under his jacket. At the time Fillmore left Boston he had been shaped merely as a pear. He was now growing into girth of Hitchcockian proportions.

When Fillmore noticed me settle into a stool at the bar, he grabbed a fresh bottle of Irish whiskey, flipped it over his shoulder, caught it behind his back—something he later confided he had never before attempted—spun around slowly, but not without grace, and handed me the bottle and a shot glass.

"Cowboy style, McGee. That's the way we do it out West."

We made the obligatory, rapid-fire exchange of personal data, and then Fillmore applied his warped but not inconsiderable mental powers to my impending financial crisis.

"Psychologist."

"Pardon me?"

"It's perfect; you can be a psychologist."

"Fillmore, you seem to forget. I dropped out of the program. I never got my degree."

"This is California, man. It doesn't matter. Anyone can be a psychologist. Officially you'll have to be something like a personal growth consultant or a life transition facilitator."

"But I don't want to be a life transition facilitator."

"It pays ninety-five dollars an hour."

"..."

"Look, it'll be easy. I've always got more patients than I can handle. I'll just refer a couple to you. Easy stuff. Bored housewives. Adjustment problems. Just sit there, you'll be fine."

It could work. Move a couple of pieces of furniture around the living room and it might look like an office. And as crazy as I knew Fillmore to be, he must know *something*. He could always step in if I got into trouble.

The next day Fillmore gave me a reprint of a recent article from the *Journal of Clinical, Counseling, and Consulting Psychology:* "And so it is our unassailable conclusion that [Fillmore's underline] <u>differences—in patients who recover, patients whose situation worsens, and patients who experience no change whatsoever—are statistically insignificant between the experimental group receiving intensive psychotherapy and the control group which received no psychological help at all.</u>"

Ninety-five dollars an hour.

FOUR

My first patient was to be Mrs. Quilp, married to one Daniel Quilp, financier. Fillmore informed me Mrs. Quilp was attractive, articulate, and, lately, depressed. In preparation I'd watched a Marx Brothers movie and skimmed a text on Rogerian psychology.

For the uninitiated among you, Rogerian therapy employs a simple, foolproof practice called unconditional positive regard. Roughly, what this means is that you convolve everything the patient says and throw it right back.

Patient: I hate my parents.

Therapist: You hate your parents.

Patient: That's right, they don't love me.

Therapist: You feel like you don't receive sufficient affection from your mother and father.

And so on.

FIVE

I was immediately taken with Mrs. Quilp. She was in her late twenties, certainly elegant, but natural. Innocent, intelligent eyes, long dark hair with interesting runs of auburn, and unmistakable evidence of personal trainers in her recent past.

A tough spot here. One reason I dropped out of graduate school was that I found out you really weren't supposed to sleep with the patients. But once Mrs. Quilp stepped into my apartment, it was impossible to ignore this matter of desire. And the fact that I had only Fillmore for backup and support did not ease the difficulty any in my mind.

"Dr. McGee Brown?"

I didn't bother to correct her. Though not a dishonest fellow, I hardly thought telling the patient I was not a doctor would begin our session on the right note.

"Please sit down."

I'd arranged the chairs in such a way as to give us both maximum comfort and to give myself the elbow support necessary to perform the psychologist's time-honored ritual of placing the fingertips of both hands together at a point just below eye level. It had been years since my last cigarette, but I'd borrowed a pipe for the day and it was conspicuously displayed.

"Now, Mrs. Quilp, how can I help you?"

"I'm in trouble."

"I see. You feel troubled."

"No, I'm really in trouble. I think my husband's trying to kill me."

"Pardon me?"

"I said I think my husband's trying to kill me."

"You think your husband's trying to kill you."

"That's right. I need help."

"You believe you need help."

"Why are you repeating everything I say?"

"What?"

"Every time I say something you repeat it right back."

"I didn't do it just now, did I?"

"No."

"All right then; don't be ridiculous."

Things were not going the way I'd hoped. Mrs. Quilp crossed her legs, the folds of her skirt falling to advantage. I grinned brainlessly and placed my fingertips together. If I were going to continue my practice, I could see it might be necessary to read another textbook.

"Daniel, my husband, is capable of anything."

"I see."

Mrs. Quilp eyed me with a trace of suspicion. I'd have to do better.

"Why do you say your husband is trying to kill you?"

"Two days ago I found a crocodile in my bedroom."

Fillmore wasn't going to believe this. On the other hand, sending me a full-blown psychotic would in no way strain the boundaries of Fillmore's sense of humor. I said the only thing that came to mind.

"How did you know it wasn't an alligator?"

"In the last forty-eight hours I've made it my business to know."

I raised my eyebrows. It was important to establish here that Mrs. Quilp was not dealing with a pushover.

"Oh, all right," she continued. "In crocodiles the long, lower fourth tooth protrudes when its mouth is closed, and the snout's narrower. But the important thing is that crocodiles are much more aggressive."

"Ah-hah."

Mrs. Quilp had been concentrating on the clasp of her purse. She looked up expectantly.

"You agree that's important. If it had been an alligator… well, I guess it's all right to show you."

She stood, turned slightly, and pulled her black linen skirt to the waist, revealing a firm, tan haunch, no bathing-suit line, and a parallel set of long, lazy cuts dotted with adhesive tape and gauze.

"I hope I'm not embarrassing you, but I had to prove I'm not making this up."

"Nonsense," I lied, "I'm quite used to this sort of thing… it's just that, it strikes me as a little unusual. You know, murder by crocodile?"

"No, that's the brilliant part. My husband keeps quite a menagerie on the grounds. Large carnivora, snakes, birds of prey."

"But surely not in the house?"

"He said it was just another new addition he'd temporarily placed in my room until its quarters were ready."

"I don't suppose it's in any way possible he's telling the truth."

"We live in a thirty-eight-room house with two guest cottages, a private zoo, and three hundred twelve acres. I can't see why he couldn't have found the crocodile adequate alternative housing."

"I see the point. Why don't you just go to the police?"

"Ha. You don't know my husband. Daniel Quilp is one of the wealthiest men in the country. Maybe the wealthiest. Certainly the most ruthless. He has a stranglehold on the police departments in a several-hundred-mile radius."

"Come now, he can't have every possible policeman in his pocket."

"I'm not saying the police are corrupt or even dishonest. But have you ever seen the way people act around incredible wealth?"

I had seen that. While covering the Monaco Grand Prix I had made an idiot of myself at every opportunity.

"Have you moved out of your house?"

At this point, Mrs. Quilp did something quite remarkable. She turned me into a professional. Briefly. She slumped in her chair, helpless, and looked to me for, well…help.

"Daniel Quilp has taken care of me since I was sixteen. I don't know what to do except stay on. I'm powerless to do otherwise."

This was the moment to take her in my arms, and I, operating under this fleeting interval of professional resolve, congratulated myself for not having done so. But as Mrs. Quilp sat there, tearful yet tempting, it became immediately obvious why all psychologists become...strange. I was pretty sure I didn't want to be a psychologist anymore, or even a life transition facilitator. I knew it wasn't ethical to become a lover, so I became the only other thing I knew how to be—a journalist.

And in the next twenty minutes, under a barrage of razor-edged interrogation from the former emerging dean of East Coast participatory journalism, I got Mrs. Quilp to reveal why she believed her husband was now trying to kill her. And in the process, I remembered something that seemed important—the people psychologists deal with are crazy.

I escorted Mrs. Quilp down the steps. She lingered in the lobby, and somewhere in the awkward silence I suggested another appointment the following day. She agreed, gratefully, I thought, and we walked out to Kearny Street.

It seems to me now that when the piano fell, I was straining to say something reassuring and psychological and profound. Fortunately, whatever I'd come up with was not interesting enough to command Mrs. Quilp's full attention. She saw it directly overhead, a fifth-floor launching, obediently observing the formula for acceleration.

She threw herself at me, on me, probably saving my life, certainly saving her own. There was a musical explosion; we lay in a clinch. A crowd gathered. The piano movers lowered their broken scaffold, apologizing all the way down. Mrs. Quilp smiled and released me.

The crowd, clucking with the communal indignation that comes automatically when someone has screwed up and you're relieved it wasn't you, dusted us off, made vague threats at the movers, and stole various piano pieces. Someone squeezed my hand. I turned to see Mrs. Quilp slide into the back seat of a Jaguar sedan.

SIX

The fifth and top floor of my building was entirely occupied by its landlords, the MahaVala Kinship Society. When I moved in, they let it be known that it was incumbent upon all tenants, in this case me, to attend an ego liberation meditation, theirs, to purge the Self of any possible offending life force, else no one in the building, specifically they, would be likely to make much spiritual progress. They were insistent and watchful, and they caught me one drunken evening and dragged me upstairs for the blessed event.

Anyone entering the temple, or as it was known to me, the fifth floor, was required to wear a set of bulky, thumbless mittens. Something about distancing oneself from the world of sensation. It seemed unlikely that a piano would suddenly fit into their plans.

SEVEN

"Hello, Stanford Medical Center."

"Dr. Fillmore, please."

"Who shall I say is calling?"

"Dr. Brown."

I'd decided by now to confer a PhD on myself whenever appropriate. A few whirrs and clicks and then…

"Dr. Brown, I presume?"

"Dr. Fillmore."

"How'd it go, man?"

"She's wild."

"Yeah. I didn't want to give her up but figured you could manage for one hour."

"No problem."

"What's her trouble?"

"Astounding relationship with her husband. Genuinely scared of him."

"He's supposed to be a scary guy. Refined, but real tough."

"She believes he put a crocodile in her room."

"Really? That's great stuff."

"She thinks he's trying to kill her."

"Uh-oh. Maybe we'd better discuss this. Uhh, I gotta split. I'm starting a group on writer's block in two minutes and...let's see, I'm booked through eight o'clock, so it'll have to be dinner. We'll celebrate your first paycheck. Cash it and I'll meet you at Vanessi's around nine. Later, man."

I'd forgotten to get paid.

EIGHT

Most of my major muscle groups let it be known they'd endured a tense afternoon. I thought I'd do one hundred push-ups and one hundred sit-ups, got to twenty-five push-ups, opened a beer, and ran a hot bath. I took the phone off the hook and spun an old tape. Preservation Hall Jazz Band. A lot of white guys had been creeping into the lineup lately, and the group seemed to be relying more on banjo.

The water was fine, but memories of the session with Mrs. Quilp began to crowd against me, and the bath lost its charm. I gave it up and went for another beer.

A thick, steady breeze came in off the bay, bouncing through Chinatown, picking up airborne particles of dim sum and MSG and stuffing them through my bedroom window. I had too many hours until dinner; a nap seemed right. Some back issues of *Sports Illustrated* and *Insanity Today* were conveniently stacked near my bed. I turned the pages, went under for a silent hour.

NINE

The maître d' at Vanessi's had decided to like me my very first night in town. He'd seen me drinking with the mayor and made certain conclusions, which he must have subsequently learned were inaccurate. But he had so much enthusiasm invested in his initial burst of goodwill that it now carried forward of its own momentum.

What happened was this. I had elbowed into the only clear space at the bar. The mayor, a not unattractive woman on my left, had been telling a particularly amusing story and found it necessary to use hand signals to clue her listeners to the most important parts. She swept her vodka and tonic into an area confirmed as unoccupied only seconds before and caught me in the side of the head. Embarrassment all around. She grabbed a cocktail napkin to repair the damage; the maître d' came around the corner to see the mayor on intimate terms, fondling actually, this guy he'd snubbed at the door a minute ago.

TEN

"Meester Magee, how good to zee you theese evening."

I smiled, something I do frequently when I can think of nothing to say but in this case because of this accent of indeterminable origin.

"Ve ave zee beeg man at your vavorite table, no? Meester Magee."

"Yes, thank you very much."

He appreciated politeness although I'm sure he would have preferred a tip. But I didn't have a "vavorite" table.

I must say I always looked forward to meals with Fillmore. He not only ate dinner, he explained it. A guided tour winding back historically through the kitchen to butchers, grocers, processing plants, farms, fishing boats, orchards, and distilleries.

Fillmore was sitting behind half a dozen empty martini glasses. Something was wrong. Had the situation been reversed, he would have lectured me about dulling my palate before a meal.

I slipped in across the table. But for the alcohol, Fillmore would have been pale. The effect was not pretty. His

19

eyes drooped into a rosy archipelago of blood vessels spiraling from cheek to jowl.

"Your phone's been busy over an hour."

"Off the hook."

"She's dead."

"Who?" But I knew.

"Mrs. Quilp. Bizarre accident. Heard it on the car radio on my way into town. They found her about six."

"What happened? Crocodile?"

"One of the animal keepers found her in the gorilla cage."

"Gorilla cage?"

Fillmore flagged down a waiter and snatched an open bottle of wine from his tray. Eyebrows were raised at the next table. The waiter looked hopefully at the maître d', shrugged, gave up his glasses, and returned to the wine cellar. Fillmore was not the sort of man to mess with in a restaurant.

"Fillmore, let's speed it up here. What the hell happened?"

"They didn't give the press too much. No explanation. Found dead."

"What was she doing in the gorilla cage? And aren't gorillas relatively docile? I don't think they're supposed to just attack without provocation."

Fillmore downed his glass, poured another. I did the same.

"She didn't have a mark on her. Apparently died of fright."

"Of fright?"

"Scared to death. Heart failure."

"Fillmore, you don't just get into a cage with a gorilla. Or I guess some people do, but not someone who turns out to be that scared of 'em."

"That's not all of it." He took a couple more swallows, these straight from the bottle. "The gorilla was dead, too."

ELEVEN

I was shocked. Mrs. Quilp, dead. Now I'd never get paid.

Fillmore and I tore into a drunken blur of garlic toast, pasta, veal chops, sweetbreads, and zabaglione. Over cognac, I resigned forever from the practice of psychology. Fillmore tipped the maître d' ten bucks, and he offered to drive us home. Nineteen seventy-nine Lincoln Continental, one headlight, radio continually poised just below the point of brain damage. "Meester Magee, zee eavy metal. Eet's too much, I love eet."

I had successfully managed to keep the most disturbing possibilities of this whole Quilp business out of my mind, but then I ran into Rana Krishna in the hallway outside my door.

He was dressed in the gold robes, purple slippers, and green skullcap befitting his status as MahaVala Kinship Society parliamentarian. A pair of thumbless mittens swung cavalierly from his belt.

Later I would discover—in one of those astounding coincidences that make you ponder the possibility of the "Great Plan"—that Rana Krishna was also Joel Siegelman.

Younger brother of Rebecca Siegelman, who now held my old job.

Had I known this at the time, I would have taken him into my apartment and shown him a shot my old photographer had recently sent along. Rebecca Siegelman on skis, seemingly paralyzed with fear, zooming into the parking lot of some unnamed winter resort, an assortment of panicked vacationers and ski instructors in her wake.

But I didn't know this at the time, so I just said, "Hey, Rana Krishna."

"Brother McGee."

The MahaVala leadership (those members with trust funds) kept a small studio apartment on my floor equipped with stereo, Cuisinart, rowing machine, popcorn maker, and large screen television.

"Who's taking piano lessons?"

He thought about this. "I give up. Fats Domino?"

"No, aren't you guys getting a piano?"

"A piano? What for?"

"You mean you weren't supposed to have a piano delivered today?"

"No, why?"

I explained, altering the details only slightly so that it was I who saved Mrs. Quilp.

"Wow. I wondered about that noise. We've been locked in silent and immobile vagary group suspension all day."

"No piano?"

"No piano. But if those movers were incompetent enough to drop the thing, maybe they were incompetent enough to get the wrong address."

"And take the trouble to haul it up five floors without checking? Nobody's that dumb."

Always on the lookout for possible converts, Rana Krishna sensed a possible opening. "Oh no?" he said, raising his eyebrows wisely. "The world's a fairly dumb place. It was just after a similar experience that I decided to retreat into the sanctuary of the MahaVala Kinship Society. December 1989. I was back East visiting my sister and…"

"I'm, sorry, R.K., I'm too beat. You can tell me some other time."

"When?"

"I don't know. Next time it comes up."

"OK."

TWELVE

Primeval fog. In the dream Mrs. Quilp enters the gorilla cage, begins to play the piano, I can't hear it because Rana Krishna has placed his mittens over my ears, Fillmore is eating glazed doughnuts. It's all unpleasant, and I'm relieved to hear the telephone.

I'd placed the phone far enough from the bed so that I had to take a waking step to reach it. Likewise the alarm clock. Holdover habits from the days when I had a real job. I swung off my pillow.

Last night's cognac throated itself, then subsided. "Hello."

"Dr. McGee Brown?"

This could only be bad. "Yes."

"Ann Adrian, executive secretary to Daniel Quilp, West Coast operations."

"Um-hm." I still had a lot of dream in me.

"Mr. Quilp would like to see you today. One o'clock."

"One o'clock?"

"Highway 101 to the Mill Valley exit, straight into Sweetwater Canyon. The street will dead-end into Quilp Valley Road. One o'clock."

THIRTEEN

"Stanford Medical Center."

"Dr. Fillmore, please."

"Who shall I say is calling?"

"Dr. Brown."

"One moment, Doctor, I believe he's with a patient."

I dragged the phone into my kitchen, fired up the espresso machine. Fillmore answered just as the steam came up to pressure.

"What?"

"I'm going to need you this afternoon."

"I've got appointments all afternoon. And I'm in with an especially lucrative client right now. Schizophrenic. I charge him separately for each personality."

"Quilp wants to see me at one o'clock."

"Shit. What for?"

"I don't know."

"What are you going to do?"

"Go, I guess. With you."

"No way, man."

FOURTEEN

Fillmore showed up shortly after noon. I filled his flask with Courvoisier and disappeared into the bedroom. Hard to select for the occasion. I settled on a blue blazer, blue button-down shirt, a quiet club tie, and jeans. We refilled the flask and were off.

Fillmore snatched a parking ticket from the Healey's windshield. I helped squeeze him into the passenger seat. The engine stuttered, then started, and we moved through traffic.

Across the Golden Gate Bridge into the mountains of Marin County.

Mt. Tamalpais is the big peak; Quilp Valley Road proved to claim a large, scenic, and strategically panoramic chunk. Quilp's estate was screened from the casual hiker or joyrider by a towering, old stone fence. The gate was open, the angles were steep. I downshifted into second, steered through a tunnel of redwood trees, and the main house came into view.

I looked at Fillmore; he was already looking at me. The only thing missing was an adjacent building for overnight accommodations and a sign that said "Bates Motel."

"Do you mind if I wait in the car?"

"Fillmore, I don't think you want to be left alone at this point any more than I do. What if the gorilla's loose?"

"The gorilla's dead."

"Yeah. *That* gorilla is."

Fillmore automatically sipped from the flask and passed it over. "OK, I'll do it."

"OK." But neither of us had moved. There was something almost palpably repellent about this place. Wide wooden steps led up to a set of enormous double doors, the front doors, black, but etched with awkward slashes and swirls. The house rose behind, its bulk blocking out the sun, forcing whatever color it might have been down to a moldy gray-green. There were peaks and gables and dormers, but the placement of each was so immediately wrong I had to turn my head.

Then the front doors opened, creaking with eerie predictability. "Dr. Brown?" A woman's voice.

"Yes?"

"Anything wrong?"

"A little car trouble. Think I've got it now."

Fillmore and I made a great fuss over undoing seat belts, setting the emergency brake, closing the doors properly, brushing dust off the hood, until we were speeded on our way by a deep roar, so close it squeaked the rattles in my dashboard.

"Panther," she said. "Feeding time."

I paused on the landing long enough to be polite.

"Ann Adrian, executive secretary to Daniel Quilp, West Coast operations."

"How do you do? This is my colleague, Dr. Fillmore."

"Dr. Fillmore. Yes. Come in. Both of you."

I could see now that what I had taken to be a design on the double doors were actually deeply carved, individual signatures. Ann Adrian was deeply carved herself. Sunken cheeks, pointed hips, long bony fingers. Strangely attractive, though, the sort of harsh beauty you might find striding the runways at Paris fashion shows.

The panther growled again; Fillmore and I raced across the threshold. It was as though we'd boarded a ship. The floor seemed to heave; my legs gave way, and I braced against some unseen force.

Ann Adrian caught me from behind, cushioned my balance against her surprisingly full breasts. "Flooring's weak here. Would have warned you, but you both moved too fast."

We turned to Fillmore. Ann Adrian, able to catch only one of us, had made the wise decision. He had fallen mightily, and it was doubtful whether three or four Ann Adrians could have done much to prevent it.

We helped him up. Once on his feet, Fillmore regained his dignity with admirable speed.

"Perhaps I can offer you two a drink? Mr. Quilp will be up presently."

"A drink. Yes, that would be fine. Dr. Fillmore, a drink?"

"Certainly."

She settled us in the library. We took opposite sides of a short, squat couch that was covered in red velour, as were several assorted chairs and a scattering of footstools. The ceiling was low; the windows, small; and the lighting, dim. It felt like an expensive whorehouse. Quilp's book collection was impressive, though—no paperbacks.

Ann Adrian returned with comically large snifters of brandy, smiled, nodded, and left. I needed both hands to maneuver the glass, but when able to do so, I discovered it contained an excellent cognac, and I warmed, having, in fact, a distinct change of heart about our upcoming meeting.

Fillmore was strangely quiet; I checked on this and found him strangely immobile also.

"Fillmore, you knock anything loose back there?"

He leaned his brow into the fingertips of one hand. "We are not alone."

I didn't like the sound of this. Had Fillmore waited until now to tell me he believed in UFOs? God? I was unable to stop myself. "You say you feel like we are not alone?"

Fillmore shot me an unfriendly glance. "There's a snake in here, man. So big you almost can't see it."

I wanted him to be wrong, badly, but there, stretched along the length of one wall, was what he described. One seldom considers snakes in terms of width, but this thing could have doubled for the Alaska pipeline.

"Dr. Brown. Dr. Fillmore."

I spun back toward the greeting and nervously, idiotically returned, "Dr. Quilp."

"Ah, you flatter me. No, not a doctor."

Quilp was all business. By that I mean he looked like he read the *Wall Street Journal*, frequently called meetings, and was at home in tall office buildings. His one breach of stereotype was a thin, trimmed mustache, which arced symmetrically into a goatee. He was tall and handsome, but aggressively so. It looked like someone had once grabbed his nose and tried to pull him through an opening smaller than his head.

But judging from the feral turn of Quilp's smile, one would hate to imagine what might have happened to a fellow who'd attempted such a thing.

"Sorry to have kept you waiting," he said in a manner that conveyed no sorrow whatsoever.

"Oh no."

"Quite all right," Fillmore put in.

"Just admiring this splendid…snake."

Quilp settled himself, perched really, on the edge of what should have been the most comfortable seat in the room. Ann Adrian returned, handed him a long-stemmed glass dangerously close to spilling over with some golden-green syrupy mess, and withdrew. He threw down half in a single swallow and unselfconsciously studied the two of us for several annoying seconds.

"We were very sorry to hear about the loss of your wife." I said this, and since it was the only possible thing left to say, Fillmore merely mumbled his assent.

"I didn't like my wife."

"No?" And again, unable to close my mouth in time, "You say you didn't like your wife?"

"I did at one time, of course, and I'm quite sure I would have again, but we'd recently been having…disagreements."

Fillmore and I shrugged psychologically.

"The usual distrust, suspicions…"

"In my experience," said Fillmore, adopting a totally counterfeit veneer of sophistication, "it's quite usual for—"

"My wife," interrupted Quilp, "had an appointment with you the day she died, Dr. Brown."

"An appointment…why yes, she did," I answered, as though this coincidence had only just occurred to me. My thoughts were connecting unpleasantly. If this man murdered his wife and thought I knew it…

"What did she say?"

"What did she say?"

"Yes, specifically, what did she say about me?"

"You?" I turned to Fillmore for support, his nose conveniently inserted deeply into his snifter.

"Well?"

"I…mm, can't…"

"What!" This unquestionably the loudest word yet spoken.

"Yes, I'm sorry, but the ethics, the *Handbook of Ethical Practice for Psychologists* is definitely explicit on this. Confidentiality. All that."

"But she's dead."

"Ah," I said, extending my imagination into the danger zone. "Now she is, yes, but not at the time in question. These cases have come up before, and ethically, regretfully, in your case…"

"Ethics." He said this in a way that made it clear we were in an area he knew little about.

"Yes, absolutely right," I thought I heard Fillmore say, although it was more a muddled, confused whine.

Quilp tossed down the remainder of his drink. I tossed down mine, but when he began to laugh I was forced to replace my last sip back into the glass, through my nose. The exact quality of the pain this caused was new in my experience, but I barely paid attention because Quilp had gotten to his feet and was shrieking like a poodle. Since I was, for the present, functioning as a psychologist, this observation fell under the classification of a professional opinion.

He regained his composure and his seat so swiftly I had to wonder whether I'd just imagined this last incident. A quick look at the quivering Fillmore confirmed all I needed to know. And just behind Fillmore, two huge men in dark uniforms had at some point slipped into place.

"All right, Dr. Brown," said Quilp, accenting the "Dr." to let me know he held the title in about as much deserving regard as I did myself.

"Since you are an intimate of my family, even privy to intimate details which I myself may not know, I'm afraid I cannot let you leave."

"What about me?" cried Fillmore, who recovered admirably and added, "I mean, what do you mean you can't let him…us leave?"

"Gentlemen, I didn't mean to alarm you. I've been under such strain. I meant that only in a manner of speaking, of course. What I really desire is to…bring you into the organization, the family of Quilp Enterprises. I'd like to hire you—right now, on the spot, to obtain your time, your services, your knowledge."

"To do what?"

FIFTEEN

Silent seconds fell. I unconsciously strained forward, caught the motion, and converted it fluidly into an examination of the ceiling.

Quilp was doing something to his face that, on top of any other body, might have been called smiling pleasantly. "Investigation."

"Investigation," returned Fillmore, as though in confirmation of his own idea.

"I believe the exact job description would be private investigator."

Emboldened by the absence of any mention of psychology, I ventured, "You want me to investigate your wife's death?"

"No!" Quilp returned angrily. "Why would I want that?"

"Why would he want that?" echoed Fillmore with even less shame than was called for. I made a mental note to volunteer Fillmore in my place at the earliest opportunity.

Quilp lowered an eyebrow threateningly. "You're never to concern yourself with that unfortunate affair. Let her memory die peacefully."

"I apologize for upsetting you. I just thought..."

"A closed chapter. Closed!"

It was my turn to say something, but I'd learned the percentage of possible successful responses was low.

"My daughter," continued Quilp, "has apparently taken my wife's death, accident, much too hard. She's disappeared. Run away from home. I want you to find her."

"Me? But I'm a psychologist." Again, to have correctly identified myself as a life transition facilitator would have required lengthy and uncomfortable explanations at this point and gained me no ground.

"I'd like you to accept the offer."

"But there must be a yellow pages full of people with more experience in these things."

"I want you."

"No, really…" I was a little confused by the sudden sweep of events, but when the various elements began to settle, the affair took shape as one that would have to continue without me. "Um, very sorry for your current difficulties…" I desperately searched for the charmed words that would get me out of there, after which time I intended to scrupulously avoid any further contact with this lunatic. "It's just not in my line."

Turning for assistance to Fillmore, I found him engaged in an unsuccessful attempt to make himself smaller. He had twisted from the locus of the conversation and was seemingly absorbed by some problem having to do with the elbow of his suit. "However," I said, watching the seams of Fillmore's jacket stretch dangerously, "there is someone who I think may be perfect for the job…"

"Ten thousand dollars now," said Quilp. "I'll cover any expenses, and fifty thousand dollars when she's returned."

"…and that someone is myself."

SIXTEEN

I had a check for ten thousand dollars in one fist, two thousand cash in the other. I was so excited I could not bring myself to let either go. To preserve dignity, I kept my hands in my pockets. Thus encumbered, I was forced to decline a second cognac, and Fillmore and I were led into the hall where two workmen were removing a heavily framed oil portrait.

Once our business arrangements had been completed, Quilp excused himself with an imperious nod and something midway between a cough and one of those laughs. Ann Adrian was again our guide through the portals of Quilp Manor.

She reached for me in what I took to be the beginnings of a caress but was actually an ill-timed move to stop a corner of the painting from hitting me in the back of the head. With no small effort, I managed to receive the blow without reflexively removing my hands.

"Sorry, sir," said one of the workmen, scanning me quickly to establish that I was not an attorney. "Uh, Miss Adrian, where should we put this?"

"Basement." She turned toward us. "It would only depress everyone now to have Mrs. Quilp's portrait hanging about."

I got a horizontal but full and direct view as the picture was hoisted for the trip downstairs. It was a face I'd never seen before.

SEVENTEEN

"But that's impossible, man."

We were on the Larkspur ferry back to town. Badly in need of murderous quantities of alcohol, we'd neither of us been able to persuade the other to drive so had done the responsible thing, proceeding directly to the boat terminal, which coincidentally was as close as the nearest bar.

Knotted layers of black clouds advanced across the bay at the same moment it occurred to me I'd left my top down. I was having a difficult time trying to figure whether this was or wasn't my day.

"Impossible or not, my dear Fillmore, that remains the fact. Either that was not Mrs. Quilp's portrait, or the woman who came to see me was not Mrs. Quilp."

Fillmore and I stood there in mutual semi shock. I'd sounded exactly like a private detective. Since I had two thousand dollars in cash, etiquette forced me to stand for our drinks, so he charitably allowed this observation to go unspoken.

But I had already discovered this private detecting business was addictive, and I watched Fillmore struggle against the realization. "All right," he said, unable to contain himself now that his deductive machinery had set in motion, "if the woman who kept Mrs. Quilp's appointment wasn't Mrs. Quilp, who was she and why would she do that?"

"I don't know, but this is kinda fun." I got another round, Fillmore commandeered a couple of window seats, and we sipped in meditative silence. Outside, the storm broke, pushing, packing most of the tourists—virtually the only other passengers on this trip running against the grain of rush hour—back into the lounge. Somehow, this thrusting, semi-soaked assemblage of camera-clutching, brightly dressed out-of-towners worked identical magic on us both, and we stood and said it at the same time.

"The daughter."

We sat again. "I do kinda like this myself," said Fillmore as I clutched my wad of bills protectively.

Fillmore went to the bathroom. I strolled the cabin, flushed, exultant over my emerging powers of detection and my pocketful of money—though in truth it was probably my inventory of cocktails.

In one corner a man sat alone. Not such a strange occurrence in itself, but in this, a suddenly crowded ferry lounge, a ring of empty seats arced around him. Sidestepping closer I leaned over for a better look into the full force of his smile.

A well-dressed man, a happy face, but full of menace, or, if not quite that, a face that got it all wrong. Like a spy from an alien planet who'd studied wardrobe, but not expression.

He turned back to Alcatraz, now passing along our starboard side. I was distracted by the squeals of several underdressed women shivering at the bar and promptly forgot the incident.

EIGHTEEN

The ferry chugged in, mated with the dock, and released its passengers. Warm city air rose to smash the incoming rain into a light fog here, making for a pleasant walk.

"Tianjin braised goat," said Fillmore. "The guy's actually from Shanxi somewhere, but the interesting part is the secret ingredient." He allowed a few moments' pause for drama. "Peanut butter."

"Peanut butter?"

"That and chunks of cinnamon bark. It's one of those rare cases where the whole is greater than the sum of its parts. Lemme make a call."

This appealed to me, chiefly because the place we had to go for it was not, strictly speaking, a restaurant, but one of those renegade establishments in the labyrinth of tunnels and basements under Chinatown. The chef, Fillmore explained, had escaped some time ago from a bloody personal affair near the border with Inner Mongolia, was smuggled across in the hold of an old opium steamer, and had hidden for years in his uncle's herb cellar not more than six blocks from where I now lived. He'd grown used to the

throbs and rhythms of life underground and even now sur-
faced rarely and only to argue with butchers and produce
dealers.

It was on one of these forays that the chef had been
delighted to discover a fat American locked in argument
with Chong the chicken man over the precise points of
color and texture he'd been fuming to raise himself. He
was further delighted that the white man was speaking in
halting but unmistakable Mandarin. Fillmore had sensed
opportunity, seized it, and became one of the few round eyes
allowed access to Chinatown's inner chambers—though for
him it was merely one stop on his grand rounds.

NINETEEN

The goat needed an hour and a half of braising, so we elected to wait it out in my apartment.

Elated by the prospect of a good dinner, Fillmore took the steps two at a time, outdistancing me and reaching my landing a whole floor ahead. I heard him gasp.

"Mr. Casbarian!"

Rounding the top step I discovered Fillmore flapping his arms at a small, balding man with a sword.

"What are you doing here?"

The man grinned, snared Fillmore's hand, and shook it. "Dr. Fillmore." And to me, "Dr. Brown?"

I, of course, made no reply to this, but Mr. Casbarian took that as affirmation and bowed formally. Punctuated with a small flourish of his scabbard, it came off quite well. Only then did he respond to Fillmore's question. "Why, your secretary arranged an appointment. As instructed by you. Enthusiastically. Confidently. Yesterday. And I'm flattered and pleased to see you both. Twenty minutes late, but as you remember, Dr. Fillmore, a man like me does not live by hard-and-fast rules and regulations either." With that he drew his sword and performed a short dance in my hallway, as though demonstrating how a man who dislikes hard-and-fast rules might behave.

"Mr. Casbarian." It sounded like a sigh, but Mr. Casbarian took it as an appeal and turned questioningly to Fillmore, who had no choice but to continue. "I'm sorry, but I need to consult with Dr. Brown in private for just a minute. Will you excuse us?"

"Certainly."

Having prepared my escape from the moment I first saw the sword, I held my key at the ready. I unlocked the door, tried to close it on Fillmore, remembered the Tianjin braised goat, and gave in. Fillmore rushed through and sank into a chair. On the other side of the wall, Mr. Casbarian seemed to be contentedly chanting to himself in a language other than English. I leaned against the door and nodded toward the sound. "Mr. Casbarian's here."

Fillmore looked up, smiled, shrugged.

"Fillmore?"

"Yes?"

"Who is Mr. Casbarian?"

"Mr. Casbarian? Um, well, did you ever see that TV show in the seventies, *Danger Man?*"

"Sure."

"He was the producer."

Fillmore sat quietly, as if that had somehow explained everything. In spite of myself, I was slightly impressed. Danger Man, after all, had been a hell of a guy—a swashbuckling, crime-fighting, girl-getting, heroic type always able to pull it off at the last minute. I'd begun to run back through my favorite episodes, but caught the motion. "Why is the producer of *Danger Man* fencing outside my door?"

"I don't know."

"You don't know?"

"I don't know why he's fencing." Fillmore puffed out his cheeks, exhaled. "I think he might be here because I referred him to you. Or told my secretary to."

"You think so?"

"I did, but I forgot. After the Mrs. Quilp thing. It derailed me."

We could hear the sound of Mr. Casbarian's sword whipping through the air trapped in my hallway, accompanied by, "Take that! And that! And that and that and that."

"Mr. Casbarian, then, is your patient?"

"No," said Fillmore carefully, "he's yours."

"Hah, out of the fucking question."

"I don't see why not, man. Now that Mrs. Quilp's dead, you don't even have one."

"Mrs. Quilp isn't dead. I mean, she is, but my patient isn't. Anyway, I'm not a psychologist anymore. I'm a private detective."

"A detective, I know, but maybe you could just…"

"Nope."

"I really thought you might enjoy him."

I considered this, cracked open the door to reveal a beaming, waving Mr. Casbarian, and closed it without comment.

"The thing is," Fillmore went on, "after running this super-character through his paces year after year, he began to believe himself superior to Danger Man, and capable of performing heroic deeds."

"You mean…"

"I'm not finished." Fillmore reached for a nearby empty glass, raised it beseechingly in my direction, but I made no move. "The great part is, he is."

"Is what?"

"Mr. Casbarian seems to have somehow—psychodynamically—grafted Danger Man's abilities onto himself."

"What exactly are you telling me?"

"In the last year he's caught a mugger and a purse snatcher, taken a black belt in tae kwon do, pulled two men from a burning building, chased down a rapist in Golden Gate Park, and bought an antique Indian motorcycle and a race-ready Morgan Plus-4, both of which he drives expertly."

"So, then, what's wrong with him?"

"He's crazy." Fillmore worked his way out of the chair, disappeared into the kitchen to make his own drink.

Back in the hallway, Mr. Casbarian's voice rose and fell as he repeatedly ran past the door shouting, "Yip, yip, yip, awaaay…" The guy was great.

I joined Fillmore, who was now fumbling with ice cube trays. "I admit he's a real catch, but I'm not doing it."

"No?" Fillmore shifted gears. "But think of poor Mr. Casbarian."

"I was; that's why I'm not doing it."

"Think how traumatic it would be to pull a switch on him now, on his therapist's very doorstep." He winced. "It's a level of rejection heretofore unknown in my experience."

"Not interested."

"Didn't you like the show?"

"That's got nothing to do with it."

"It pays ninety-five dollars an hour."

"Don't need it."

"Maybe he could get you in the movies."

TWENTY

"Now then, Mr. Casbarian, what seems to be the trouble?"

At the mention of the word *trouble*, he lowered his eyebrows and surveyed the room suspiciously. Madness, however, had already widened his eyes beyond hope of recall, so this last maneuver, designed no doubt to cast fear over all he surveyed, merely made him look like Richard Nixon furiously attempting to stifle a sneeze.

We were in the restaurant/home of Fillmore's chef pal somewhere under Chinatown, where Mr. Casbarian had correctly identified our meal as Tianjin braised goat without being told. He'd accepted the unorthodox circumstances of our first session with delight, extending his good feelings to the point of insisting upon paying the bill.

His sword, which had caused no small amount of commotion as we made our way to dinner, was checked with our coats and received without commotion once we arrived. ("Saber, actually. Broadsword. Cavalry sword. Cutting edges. Triangular blade. No slicing below the belt.")

Mr. Casbarian had spent the afternoon dueling, though as student, teacher, or settling a point of honor he'd not made clear. I watched him attack the food, charm the waiters, and drink as much as Fillmore.

He was pudgy, very pink, and given to wearing things like belts with knives concealed in the buckle, watches able to tick at any height or depth on the planet, and tear-gas-shooting pens. Demonstrations of these various fashion accessories kept me entertained throughout dinner, but it was time to get to business.

"Mr. Casbarian?"

"Yes."

"I said, what seems to be bothering you?" My strategy was to control the conversation, sound him out on the movie thing as quickly as possible, and then somehow pawn him off, back on Fillmore.

"My problem, you mean?"

"Yes, your problem, the one that emerged after you left show business."

The arc of his smile tightened, but only slightly. "I've been shipwrecked on the voyage of self-discovery."

"What?" (Rogerian school instinctively abandoned here.)

"Not really shipwrecked, of course. I don't even own a boat…"

Mr. Casbarian was lost to us for a few moments as the various possibilities for self-revelation inherent in boat-buying occupied his thoughts.

"Mr. Casbarian?"

"Yes?"

"Go on."

"Oh, well, you know, existential neurosis. What's it all about? Where are we going? What am I doing? Why do it?"

All good questions. But I thought it best to zero in on something relatively tangible. "I see. Now, why exactly did you leave Hollywood?"

"Artistic differences."

I'd heard of these. "Understandable for a man of your obvious sensitivities, Mr. Casbarian, but did you, for example, have the power, the...uh...artistic control to...oh, I don't know...cast an actor you chose for a particular role?"

"It wasn't that."

"But can you do it? I mean, could you have done it?"

"You feel my Hollywood experience is important." Mr. Casbarian tugged thoughtfully at his left cheek. "Don't you want to hear about the time I sneaked into Tibet?"

"Definitely, but later. I think we're onto something already. Could you, even now, just pick up the phone and..."

"The thing was, I wanted to make the show more cerebral. I'd discovered the physical stuff ran thin quite quickly."

"Yes. But..."

"I wanted to do an episode where Danger Man confronts the fact that he's always surrounded by trouble and having to kill people, and perhaps he steps out of character and theorizes that most TV heroes would be Jonahs in real life, with murder, drugs, robbery, and kidnapping always nipping at their heels."

Interesting point. "Interesting point."

"Yet every time I went to script with an idea like that, you know, one with merit, I found myself penciling in scenes where Danger Man is hit in the face with custard pies. What does that all mean?"

We were interrupted just then by a graceful waitress we'd not seen before. Dark, waist-length hair, darker eyes, wearing a fragile, unsashed white robe that fell open against a soft, engaging display of the palest lemon. And bearing a tray of assorted vials, jars, bottles, and beakers.

She woke Fillmore, who'd been dozing, flirted with Mr. Casbarian, and wiped my face and shoulders with a damp silk cloth. Then, working swiftly from her portable lab, she concocted us each a cordial—Fillmore's purple, mine sort of a British racing green, and Mr. Casbarian's a layered red, white, and blue.

Then there was laughter. Mr. Casbarian performing magic tricks, other tables sending over desserts, other tables sending envoys, Mr. Casbarian lecturing on the Ghost Dance of the Dakota Indians, Fillmore doing it, other diners doing it, other tables pushed next to ours, the waitress making a second round, a song, more laughter, more drinking, some face painting, smoking, more dessert...

TWENTY-ONE

Telephone. Hangover. Went toward the ring obediently. Hated myself for doing it. Must get answering machine. Softly, "Hello."

"Dr. Brown?"

"Shit."

"Pardon?"

"It...is he."

"Ann Adrian, executive secretary to Daniel Quips, West Coast operations."

"Umh, hello."

"Mr. Quilp asked me to inquire as to your plans."

"My...?"

"How you intend to find his daughter, spend his money."

"Money, yes. Excuse me, a late night. Just waking."

A pause on her end, presumably giving me time to wake. At this point, my only plan had been to maximize Quilp's offer to "cover all expenses."

"Dr. Brown...?"

"Ms. Adrian."

"I've prepared a dossier that may be of some use. Recent photographs, friends, places she may have gone."

51

"Yes, I was planning to call you asking for just that."

"Shall we say lunch?"

"Lunch? Fine." I could probably manage the three blocks to Enrico's. "Enrico's?"

"One o'clock."

She rang off. I needed coffee. Aspirin. Did I have these things? What time was it? What kind of a day was it? For the answer to these and other questions, I decided to wake up with some finality.

I pushed out the bedroom door, stumbled over something in the hall, took several lunging steps, and crashed loudly into a coffee table that should have been at least three feet to the left.

"Dr. Brown?"

"Mr. Casbarian! What are you doing?" I saw what he was doing. Sleeping with the beautiful waitress on my floor. In a far corner, her silk robe hung from the hilt of Mr. Casbarian's sword.

"I'm sorry, Doctor, but I thought last night..."

"No, I'm sorry. Half-asleep. Going for coffee. Please ignore the interruption." Let's see, there had been some talk leaving the restaurant, *esprit de corps,* fellowship, comradeship, but even now, it still had all the qualities of a dream.

"I should get up and prepare you a bowl of Mato Grosso maté. Always carry it." Mr. Casbarian raised on an elbow. "I myself need only two hours sleep a night, but I've not had quite that..." A delicate hand snaked from the blankets, caught much of what there was of Mr. Casbarian's hair, and reclaimed him.

TWENTY-TWO

The staff at Enrico's inexplicably assumed me to be Fillmore's brother, and I was treated with familial familiarity—larger drinks, special dishes, special tables, philosophical discussions with Enrico, and all the coffee I could drink.

I chose an outdoor table in Kermish's section where he presented me with a cup of Kermish's crazy Kahlua cognac coffee. At three minutes past one, a blood red Chrysler limousine double-parked across the street. Ann Adrian let herself out, jaywalked purposefully through traffic, and nodded to the driver, who sped away.

She wore endangered species skins tightly molded off one shoulder to midthigh. The swells of voluptuousness I'd suspected at our previous meeting were presented now without ambiguity.

I pulled out a chair. She sat down, award-winning posture, and unslung a black leather portfolio. Behind the bar, a small scuffle broke out among the waiters as the boundaries of Kermish's territory were hotly debated.

"Dr. Brown."

"Ms. Adrian."

She allowed the trace of a smile to catch her features. Kermish emerged, rumpled. I watched him watch her, then, remembering the expense account, suggested cocktails.

"Vodka martini, straight up, extra olives."

Bourbon seemed right for a private investigator, so I ordered that.

"I've organized the material we discussed," she stated, withdrawing a number of manila envelopes from the portfolio, which now occupied most of our table. "I'm operating on the theory that Qina's not a very courageous woman, and it's likely she'd flee to some known spot."

"Qina Quilp?"

"Yes, her father forbade her to take her husband's name."

"She's married?"

"Once. A regrettable affair. Mr. Quilp soon broke it up. A writer. You know the type. Charming, a lot of spirit, but entirely disreputable. She's quite alone now."

"Could she have gone back to him?"

"Oh no. He's dead."

I was sure there was a story in that, but I'd been handed a stack of photographs. Qina smiling. Qina pensive. Qina on horseback. Qina at the governor's mansion. Qina in the *Chronicle*, Qina in *W, Vanity Fair*, the *New York Times*. Qina yachting—a bathing suit here, good for identifying marks. No crocodile claw lines, but these were the same legs, and this, my patient.

The next item on the agenda appeared to be a list of real estate offerings—large colonials in Washington, Boston, and Philadelphia; a manor house outside London; mixed-breed estates in Chicago, Cleveland, Kansas City,

Denver, Los Angeles; a six-bedroom, six-bath apartment on the Avenue Foch in Paris; a New Orleans Garden District plantation; a penthouse, Central Park West.

"Mr. Quilp hates hotels." Ann Adrian finished her drink, capturing, teasing the last olive between her teeth. Slow squirts of vodka spilled thickly onto her lower lip. I stared, as surprised and absorbed as if she'd just caught a bullet. "I'm sorry." She chewed. "Martinis make me a bit crazy."

Kermish, eavesdropping, went inside to fetch another round. Ann Adrian lit a squat, unfiltered cigarette. Black tobacco, a fitting olfactory backdrop because I'd now reached the exotic section—villas, chalets, lodges, a white-washed palace in New Delhi, another in Tangier, a summer home in Death Valley, a finca near a small Amazon river port called Lomalito, a houseboat in Bangkok, a ranch in Kenya... How could Quilp ever remember in which closet he'd left which shirt?

"I know this doesn't terribly narrow things down for you, but I took my list of her friends..." she paused long enough to find that, pass it, "...and correlated the two."

The top name on Qina's "friend list" was Gabrielle Dupuy, a French actress I could actually recall playing a leading role in certain of my dreams. Checking Ann Adrian's synthesis file, I was happy to see Paris had survived the cut.

"Well, if Qina's simply gone to one of the family homes, wouldn't it be easy enough to phone doormen or caretakers or neighbors to see if she's there?"

Ann Adrian looked at me uncomprehendingly. "That's why he hired you."

"Of course. Just thinking out loud. Uh, is there a chance that's all there is to it?"

"Depends whether Qina's hiding from her father or just wants be left alone."

I couldn't remember ordering, yet lunch nonetheless arrived—Enrico flourishing two plates of angel wing pasta, and Kermish struggling with the cork on a murky bottle of Chianti.

Ann Adrian raised an approving eyebrow behind the obligatory shower of pepper and Parmesan. She ate with enthusiasm, healthy, farm-girl, bites, liberal quaffs of wine. I knew I should question her further about Qina, I knew I should plan various avenues of seduction, but the issue of Quilp's wealth was overpowering. It was odd that I'd never heard of him.

"Few people have." She refilled our glasses. "A very few beyond staff could tell you what he looks like. Never socializes." Topping a shaving of French bread with enough butter for half the loaf, dumping a spoonful of Parmesan onto that: "I myself have never seen a single photograph."

The trick with angel wings is to steep and swirl each in the deepest puddle of sauce, then deliver it to your mouth as quickly as possible. If the distance is too great, a splash factor comes into play; too short, and one looks like an ill-mannered Neanderthal. Ann Adrian balanced bites on the end of her fork and splattered indifferently.

"Your appointment was something of a rarity," she continued, licking a drop from her forearm. "Donald Trump's never had a phone call returned."

"How'd he make his money, Quilp?"

"Buying, selling, building, tearing down, foreclosing, speculating, manipulating."

The portfolio rang. She disinterred a gold cordless telephone, lengthened the aerial, and sneaked a quick sip of wine. "Ann Adrian...for you, Dr. Brown."

I checked to make sure Kermish and Enrico were watching, ostentatiously cleared my throat: "Brown here."

"Hold please for Daniel Quilp."

"Certainly."

"Brown!"

Reduced almost immediately, I reflexed, "Where are you?" as though I were some bushman expecting to find him hiding under the table.

"If you must know, I'm on my way to the airport. Why?"

"Oh, I just was, uh, hoping you could join us."

"Ha ha ha ha."

"Ha ha ha."

"Ha ha, what progress?"

"Progress, yes, a lot, I think. I've been analyzing Ms. Adrian's dossier."

"And?"

"Uh, Paris."

"Paris!"

"Yes." I went after the Chianti in gulps. "I admit there's an element of hunch here, but Ms. Adrian and I have discussed the matter at some length..."—a quick smile, and I drew her into conspiracy—"...and we agree Paris is a logical first attempt."

A thick slice of hair disengaged, Veronica Laked across one eye. Her nose quivered slightly, and beneath, her lips, full and savory and smiling.

"You do? All right then. Ms. Adrian will arrange travel."

Quilp clicked off.

Ann Adrian measured me through half-closed eyes. She took the receiver, her hand lingering against mine a beat longer than necessary. "It's not often that I see anyone… handle Daniel Quilp."

If I could keep my mistakes at a minimum, I'd have Ann Adrian tonight, France this time tomorrow. Elbows on the table, she leaned in close, a breast lowering dangerously near the topmost rise of pasta.

"Well, I wouldn't exactly say…" Something in her eyes registered I was making a wrong turn. Ann Adrian was not the sort to be much affected by modesty.

"Dr. Brown."

"Ms. Adrian."

She relaxed back into a smile. "You're an unusual man." This could mean anything. "You live somewhere nearby, am I correct?" But this was clear. "Brandy in stock?"

"Yes."

A dramatic pause. She turned from the action, fussed momentarily with some internal arrangement in the portfolio. "Why don't we finish this at your place?"

TWENTY-THREE

Mr. Casbarian.

But he was gone, wonderful. And he had cleaned up the apartment, better.

Ann Adrian settled into my couch; I went for the cognac. On the door of my refrigerator, a memo—

from the escritoire of A. Casbarian

~~Warner Brothers~~

~~Pindar~~	~~Tribes~~
~~Wheel of Existence~~	~~Gofan~~
~~lunch~~	~~Motilone~~
~~clean sheets~~	~~Djuka~~
~~Hamsters~~	

~~Nuclear Regulatory Commission~~

See you next week

A.C.

"Dr. Brown?"

I'd lost several moments going over the last entries. Was Mr. Casbarian planning some nuclear adventure? Was he possibly on the Nuclear Regulatory Commission? Were the hamsters slated for sacrifice to the reenactment of some primitive, pagan ritual? To lunch? "Just coming." I grabbed glasses, joined Ann Adrian.

"It was nice of you to make room for us in your schedule, Doctor. I'm quite sure Mr. Quilp will be more than generous in his appreciation."

I put down my snifter, placed my fingertips together. "I felt empathy for the man."

"Empathy. For Daniel Quilp?"

"For his situation."

"I see."

I felt she didn't. Understandable in the face of such monumental distortion of truth. Change of direction was better than trying to dig myself out. "How did you come to work for him?"

She sighed. I'd either begun to establish a sense of intimacy, touching, sensitively probing a life-changing issue, or asked a boring question. "Daniel Quilp saw a cover I'd done for *Vogue*. He bought up my contract, sent me through NYU business school. In style."

"You were a model, then?" No, she was a plumber.

"Yes. But as we all know, a job with a limited future. So, I sold my soul to Quilp Enterprises. Never looked back."

We strayed into an awkward silence, but I felt sure that the slow, irreversible slide to seduction had begun in those last moments of lunch. Events were proceeding. I lubricated us both with second cognacs.

Ann Adrian drank hers straight through, set her glass on the coffee table, held it as though punctuating the moment. She turned toward me, shifted a shoulder. The endangered species skins peeled back, released apparently by a single, hidden hooklet.

A small tattoo on her left breast, a portrait of herself. Anyone that vain has got to be great, or at least pretend that she is, which amounted to the same thing for my purposes.

There was moisture on her upper lip, moisture on her brow. I impulsively tasted it, eliciting a low moan. She stroked, nibbled, heated the length of my neck, and side to side. I ran my hand under her dress; she tensed, adjusted to make room. Ann Adrian was copiously supplied, her legs richly charged, her ass round and forgiving, ripples under her stomach, and all of it steadily warmer. She pushed lace panties below her knees, toed out the rest of the way.

I explored enthusiastically, deep into the dizzy region of her thighs. She spread her legs, moved her hand inside my buttons and zippers, pressing, twisting. The smell was of some exotic, freshly cut forest.

A knock at the door.

A long kiss, pulling me in close, moving down my chest. More knocking. On me now, her fingers squeezing, pulsing in my back pockets.

Pushing hard, squirming, throwing herself into me in steady, thrusting rhythms. Legs curled, holding, climbing up my side.

The doorbell now, without stop. We slowed, waited. Bell and knocking in concert.

Ann Adrian drew herself up, found the bedroom on her own. I rebuttoned, tucked, zippered, and opened the door.

Rebecca Siegelman.

"Brown. There you are. I thought I heard someone in there."

Rebecca Siegelman. Sports columnist. Participatory journalist. Holder of my old job.

"What's wrong with you, Brown? It's me, Rebecca."

"Rebecca…"

TWENTY-FOUR

Headache: Pain…intracranial pressure…throbbing…many causes including emotional tension…
—*Pratt & Prager's Encyclopedia of Medical Terminology*

"Why are you holding your forehead?"

"Rebecca." One arm was in a paisley sling, and a bandage hung over the left eye. But there was a new spot of color in her cheeks, and she may have dropped just a pound or two. "What are you doing here?"

"I'm in town on a story. Staying at Campton Place."

The best hotel in the city. And a round-trip to California. All on my old expense account. True, it was nothing when weighed against my current expense account, but at their worst, my editors had been cub scouts compared to Quilp. Better to keep in touch in case Rebecca breaks her neck. I'll drop them a postcard from Paris. Hah!

"Brown."

"Yes, what?"

"Can I come in?" She did.

"Um, I guess. How did you manage to knock and ring the bell at the same time?"

She came back through the doorway, smiled, something I'd never before seen her do, threw her hip into the bell, and knocked my forehead with her uninjured hand.

"Rebecca, please. I have a headache."

"Sorry." She flopped on the couch. Or what was left of it. Cushions were scattered all over the room. "Housekeeping not your strong suit, Brown?"

"Hmh." I sat on the coffee table. "What happened to you?"

"Skiing accident."

Oh yeah. That photograph. I laughed without thinking.

"You find skiing accidents funny, Brown?"

"No, no, no. Just kind of laughing at life. You know, how I wound up here, you still back where I used to be, how nice it was to see an old face, er, friend." How to get her out of here as quickly as possible?

"No hard feelings? I mean, about me having your old job and all."

"Nah."

Rebecca took in the room. "Where's your wife?"

I'd almost forgotten that chapter of my affairs. "Things didn't really work out. Never got married, actually."

"Yeah. I heard something like that. Sorry." Music was turned on in the bedroom. KJAZ.

Rebecca stood. "Didn't realize you had company." She made for the door.

This was good, but jealousy forced me to slow her departure. "What piece are you working on out here?"

"Backgammon." She raised her sling. "This has kept me out of real action pretty much, so I'm doing a series on gambling. Poker, darts, craps, like that."

Not a bad idea at all. "Who are you playing?" Please not Easy Money.

"Easy Money."

Easy Money. I always meant to get around to him. Fat, flamboyant, and lucky, he plowed through tournaments like a blunt weapon. A country con man in a country club sport, enough there for a three-part series.

The accompanying photos clicked in my mind. Easy with his pint-sized Korean wife. Easy holding court in Vegas, on his houseboat in Sausalito, in his customized Cadillac van complete with Captain Kirk's chair from an old set of *Star Trek*.

"Brown?"

"Yes, what?"

"I'll see you."

"Right, uh, hey, there are some really good high school athletes out here. All-Americans."

"High school athletes?"

"Yeah…you know, that world, those high-stakes gamblers. Late nights. I just thought if it got too rough for you… good story and all, but…"

"Geez, Brown. Didn't know you cared." She punched me affectionately on the shoulder. "I'll be OK. I may not be a lot of things, but I'm a pretty good sport."

Guess maybe she was. "Good-bye, Rebecca."

"Bye, Brown."

She ambled down the hall, taking my career with her. Well, what did I care? I was off to Paris.

TWENTY-FIVE

Ann Adrian greeted me with hot, sibilant whispers on the topic of our immediate future. She was now completely unclothed save a thin strand of diamonds at the throat. There was something almost reptilian in her approach— slithering, coiling, hypnotic. And underneath it all the quick, sure coordination of a circus performer.

TWENTY-SIX

I woke in the dark. A slice of headache, clearly a memory surge of Rebecca's visit, and cramps in the small of my back. I straightened my legs, twisted out some of the pain.

My association with Quilp Enterprises had begun rather grandly, I thought. I was alone in bed, but Ms. Adrian's clothes still lay smoothed over my dresser. Eight thirty. She was probably scanning the refrigerator, planning my dinner.

I thought I'd surprise her. Tipping, toeing to the door. The notion of the two of us naked in my kitchen rendered me lightheaded, and I redoubled my efforts to slow and steady my pace.

Pushing softly through the door, into the hall. Around the corner, a light on over my desk. Ann Adrian nude in my chair. The effect was far more erotic than anything I'd imagined in the kitchen, but I was left unmoved because Ms. Adrian was quite obviously going through the contents of my drawers.

I pulled back, then peeked again. She hadn't seen me, and I hadn't been wrong. I watched her sort, stack, and speed-read the contents of one drawer, replace them and go for another.

My move here was to do nothing. A) The papers in my desk were of no value. Probably not even to me if I really thought about it. B) By not alarming her I'd have a better chance of discovering what she was up to, assuming this was not simply a manifestation of some personal insanity. C) I didn't want to jeopardize my chances of sleeping with her again. D) Must maintain cordial, uncluttered lines to the expense account.

I crept back into the bedroom, lay in the sheets. The scent of her was strong and unadulterated by perfume.

What the hell was she doing? Probably just part of some routine security check Quilp runs on all his employees. Of course, if this were true, it greatly lessened the odds on a sexual future here.

That made me angry. I changed the radio to KFOG, turned it up (the Rolling Stones yelling about something), opened and closed the closet door.

Ann Adrian appeared in seconds. "Dr. Brown." She stepped to her clothes with obvious intent. "I want to thank you for a very rewarding session, Doctor." Underwear and stockings were stuffed in her portfolio, the cordless phone came out. "Ready now, Dennis. Brown's apartment."

She slid into her dress and kissed me good-bye, one hand stroking my forehead, the other, briefly between my legs. "Pick your flight and hotel tonight, phone it into our service. I'll drop off tickets and such in the morning."

I leaped to my desk the moment she was gone, quickly realized it might take hours to determine if anything was missing, took a shower.

TWENTY-SEVEN

I called Fillmore. He brushed aside the Ann Adrian incident, save a few anatomical curiosities he felt he must satisfy, but I had his attention.

"Paris!?"

"Where should I stay?"

"Paris. And Quilp's buying. This is turning out all right, man."

"Run through the best hotels, something great, but don't push it."

"I'm coming."

"To Paris?"

"Why not?"

"What about your patients?"

"Oh yeah…aah, I'll work something out. Probably be good for most of them."

"I don't know, Fillmore."

"Hey, I'm responsible for this, remember?"

Words he would live to regret. "Where was this enthusiasm at Quilp's house yesterday?"

"It was there. I just felt…under the circumstances…I did come, didn't I?"

"If I let you in on this, do you promise to reveal the locations of all those secret little restaurants you brag about?"

"My Parisian friends would string me up, man."

I said nothing.

"All right. Yes. I promise."

"You're in."

"Great. OK, let's stay at the…"

"Wait a minute. Just run through them. I pick."

"I know which one you'll pick in the end."

"Do it anyway." Best to establish myself quickly before Fillmore ran away with the whole deal.

"OK. The rich are at the Plaza-Athénée, but the most expensive is the Bristol. The George V has the best views, the Saint-James et Albany the best location, and the Royal Monceau's got the nicest rooms." In his excitement, Fillmore had grabbed something on his end and begun to chew between phrases. "The Crillon is the most French, but the French never stay there. You can't go wrong at the Ritz or the Intercontinental, and if you want to shoot pool, it's the Nova Park Elysées."

I waited. Fillmore's underdeveloped sense of theater demanded, predictably, that he hold back his real choice till last.

"So, you can pick from one of those, or you can stay on the Left Bank at the quiet, old, elegant Hotel Monjauze where Hemingway used to sneak off to screw Gertrude Stein."

"Never happened."

"Would you like to see the photographs?"

"Hemingway and Gertrude Stein?"

"You won't find it in the bios, but those two monstrous egos decided to record their coupling in some detail. The album's in a vault in the basement."

I was usually lukewarm on pornography, but this sounded more interesting than billiards.

"There's a nonstop at noon," Fillmore continued. "I'll reserve two, pick you up in the morning."

TWENTY-EIGHT

I beat my alarm, dressed quickly, phoned Ms. Adrian's assistant with plane and hotel information, and ran the three blocks to catch Enrico arriving behind an armload of produce. He emptied half the kitchen into an omelet, and we split a bottle of Dom Pérignon to celebrate my departure.

Ran home. Packed. Still a couple of hours to go. Ran to the Trieste for coffee. Ran to City Lights for a traveling book. Hemingway? Stein? Toklas? Maybe something general on Paris?

"Buy this." The clerk had come out from behind the counter.

"*A Guest in the Jungle?*" I flipped the pages. "I wanted something for a trip to Paris. This takes place in the Amazon jungle."

"It's the best book in the shop."

"OK. Wrap it up."

Ran home. Moved my suitcase three inches closer to the door. Checked my watch. Straightened up a bit. Turned down the thermostat. Left a note for the mailman.

A knock on the door. Visions of Rebecca briefly resurfaced.

"Dr. Brown."

"Ms. Adrian."

"How are you?"

"Fine. Fine. You?"

"The same. I have some very good news for you."

"Yes?" Why do people always follow a tantalizing line like that with a pause? She handed me a set of car keys. I turned them over in my hand. "I'm driving to France?"

"We have a very solid lead on Qina. It seems she's at the summerhouse in Death Valley. I thought you'd need slightly more practical transportation."

Qina? Of course. My job. My case. I'd totally forgotten about her. "What was that about Death Valley?"

"Mr. Quilp keeps a home there, but it usually stands empty. We bring staff in with us." She lit a cigarette, exhaled, aiming in the direction of my bedroom. "The local sheriff runs a gas station in Furnace Flats. He filled up Qina's car, reported in."

"Reported?"

"Just a routine courtesy call." She handed me an envelope. The Transcendent Travel Agency. Inside, a memo. Two first-class, round-trip tickets to Paris, two suites at the Hotel Monjauze, both entries X-ed out, and beneath, directions to Death Valley Junction.

"Unfortunately," she continued, "there's no direct route in. You go south to Bakersfield, then cut back north for the desert."

"Bakersfield."

"That's right. Now, listen carefully. Bring plenty of water. The outside temperature's going to be hotter than you are, so you'll sweat about a quart an hour. I brought you some things…"

The portfolio again. She pulled out a ridiculous crushed sombrero, goggles, and a long-sleeved L.L. Bean safari shirt, put them in my arms. "Never walk outside without these."

My mind was still not working properly. Images of myself strolling down the Champs Elysées in goggles and a sombrero struggled mightily on the internal tides.

"I got you a Jeep Cherokee," Ms. Adrian went on, "four-wheel drive. It's parked below. If you become bogged down in the sand, try deflating the tires a bit."

"Bogged down."

"Right. A lot these roads are hardly used. If you break down, it could be weeks before someone happens by."

"Weeks…anything else?"

"Flash floods this time of year. You can see for miles, so watch for storm clouds over the mountains."

"Anything else?"

"Wind. It picks the hot air layers off the ground."

"Anything else?"

"Yes. When you bring Qina back, you'll be fifty thousand dollars more attractive." She moved in to kiss me, but the sombrero proved a formidable obstacle, and the moment was lost. "House key is the big iron one."

"Got it."

"That's all then." She opened the door herself, scanned the living room. "Too bad you're alone. The desert is much safer for two."

TWENTY-NINE

"Fillmore! How ya doin'?"

"Never better, man." He put down his valise and a huge leather briefcase I knew to be full of lunch. No matter how first the class, airline food was airline food. "What's with the sombrero?"

"Just putting a few things in order." A delicate matter here. If I could get Fillmore to Death Valley, he'd be sure to notice the absence of cafes, Citroens, the fact that people were still speaking English; but I knew once there, he'd resign himself to the situation. "How about a quick Bloody Mary?"

He consulted his watch. "I guess we have time, but you never know how long it's going in take to get a cab."

"Cab! Oh no. We're taking my new car."

Fillmore raised a finger threateningly. "I'm not relying on your Austin Healey to get us to the airport."

"No, really, I've got a new car. Jeep Cherokee. Dependable. Plenty of room for luggage."

"Spending your money already. I like that confidence. Bloody Marys it is, man."

The psychologist in me was free of guilt; he'd voluntarily canceled his patients. I calculated Fillmore's weight in Valiums, crumbled them in tomato juice, added black pepper, red pepper, celery salt, Worcestershire, Tabasco, lemon, basil, thyme, and Stolichnaya. (The Russians were well out of Afghanistan, and I thought it was time to stop teaching them a lesson.)

I experienced a pang of remorse when Fillmore raised his glass and shouted, "To Paris!" but I settled it with a straight vodka of my own.

Timing was everything. I had to get him to the car before the drug took effect or I'd never be able to maneuver him down the steps.

In the kitchen, I poured his remaining Bloody Mary mix into the Stolichnaya bottle. I then emptied every jar in my refrigerator and filled them all with water.

"Monsieur! Monsieur?"

"Yes, Fillmore?" I found him dancing a little cancanière in the hallway. He was beginning to drool.

"*Allons-y.*"

"*Oui, un moment.*"

I dragged my suitcase into the bedroom, pulled out everything respectable, crammed in a few lightweight shirts, khakis, and a pair of jeans.

Fillmore had drifted into an extremely bad impersonation of Maurice Chevalier.

"C'mon, Fillmore."

"Eef a nightingale could zing like…OK. Leez get it on." He grabbed the handle of his valise in what proved to be the first move of a rather nicely executed somersault. "Oof."

I helped him back to his feet. "Wow, guess I musta been too up to get much sleep last night. Drink's really hittin' me."

"Let me get you down to the car." I put my left shoulder under his right, snared his wrist. We stumbled through my front door, accelerating down the hall into the far wall, stacking up this way—Fillmore, me, Rana Krishna, the wall.

"Ow!"

"Rana Krishna. How's it going?"

"I can't move."

"Just a second." I managed to prop Fillmore against the corner. "Can you give me a hand?"

"Uh, I guess so." He straightened his vestments.

Rana Krishna and I proved a good team. Keeping our zigging and zagging at a minimum, we descended with increasing speed, realizing our mistake only as we hit street level.

The top of Fillmore's body had somehow arrived in advance of his bottom half. As he lost his balance beyond all hope of recovery, Rana Krishna and I, each caught helplessly under an armpit, accompanied him in a headlong rush toward the row of parked cars, sweeping an unlucky pedestrian along for the ride—the mayor.

Fillmore smelling of drink, Rana Krishna in his robes, and I, though only recently disheveled due to my tribulations with the Falstaffian Fillmore, disheveled nonetheless; we three looking for all the world like a hack cartoonist's rendition of conventioneers emerging from an all-night bacchanalia. The only spot of good fortune in the whole incident was that the car against which we were now squashing the senior executive of the city of San Francisco was my own new, purple Jeep Cherokee.

When we disentangled, she gave Rana Krishna's outfit the once-over, gaped fearfully at our reeling Fillmore, and stared hard, trying to place me as I made muffled apologies with a hand over my face, pretending to comfort the bridge of my nose.

Mustering as much dignity as circumstances would allow, she strode off beneath Fillmore's all too meretricious rendition of "Zank 'Eaven for Little Girls."

We stuffed Fillmore in the back seat, returned upstairs for the luggage. To his credit, Rana Krishna accepted an armload of water jars, the sombrero, and the goggles without comment, and deposited it all in the rear cargo section.

"Thanks, R.K. Couldn't have done it without you."

Our eyes met, his hiding a hundred questions. I could tell he was dying to come along wherever it was we were headed. One could almost hear the precepts of the Maha Vala Kinship Society slip from their cerebral moorings. I think it was the goggles that intrigued him most, but he said only, "Have fun," patted the Jeep affectionately, pulled on his thumbless mittens, and walked slowly back to his temple.

All right then. Death Valley it was. Not quite Paris, but fifty thousand dollars for a few days' jaunt left little room for complaint.

Across the Bay Bridge, 580 out of Oakland, and on to Highway 5. A straight shot down to Bakersfield, then east and north through the Greenhorn Mountains, Miracle Hot Springs, past Bald Eagle Peak, Bodfish, and the Sequoia Forest, a hard left to the north between China Lake Naval Weapons Center and the L.A. Aqueduct, Lower Haiwee Reservoir, Upper Haiwee Reservoir, east to Panamint Springs and the desert.

Ms. Adrian had neglected to lay in a stock of cassettes, but the radio was state-of-the-art—flat black controls, luminous green readouts, and a scanner-seeker that served me well.

There was trouble in the Middle East, a failed coup in Central America, dire drought predictions for the Sahara, a politician laughing off an indictment, the Chicago Cubs and the Cleveland Indians launched inevitably into their midsummer dives, and sunshine all day for California.

In an attempt to get into the spirit of my Jeep, I began with country-western music but switched to "Oldies but Goodies" for most of the ride.

Fillmore had slipped off the seat, splayed out like some boneless troglodyte, but he looked content, and in a charitable turn, I adjusted the various airflow controls to his advantage.

Ms. Adrian's dossiers lay in the passenger seat. The road was straight; the traffic, light; and I was able to flip through my Qina material and let the wheel alignment do the principal steering.

I consulted her "friend list" for Death Valley. Nobody. This made sense on two counts. First, she was probably interested in a safe, undisturbed haven in which to sort through her thoughts, and second, as far as I knew, nobody much must live in Death Valley anyway, friend or stranger.

The photos of Quilp's desert retreat were remarkable. It looked something like Mad Duke Ludwig's Bavarian monsterpiece, something like the Alamo, the clash of styles incorporated incongruously into a sprawling, twisted giant in the middle of nowhere.

THIRTY

Around two thirty I pulled into a rest stop and opened Fillmore's briefcase. Half a roasted capon, two baguettes and a Parmesan brioche, a bottle of Stag's Leap Cabernet '73, a smoky flask of Armagnac, shakers of salt, pepper, basil, oregano, and rosemary, a vial of olive oil, and a miniature cooler with slices of caper-studded, coral red salmon, a lemon, two tomatoes, a chunk of buffalo mozzarella, a disk of chèvre, a wedge of Stilton, a container of mysterious black olives, another of leeks vinaigrette, a d'Anjou pear, grapes, rare strips of lamb with an accompanying dark mustard sauce, a split of Domaine Chandon, and a spongy tiramisu for dessert.

I raised my first glass in his honor, had at least one taste of everything, several of most, repacked it all carefully, as I was heading into lean country, loosened Fillmore's tie, fired up my engine, and merged into traffic with renewed optimism.

Fillmore woke just once, in the last moments of dusk, on a bump just past the spur road to Darwin.

"Brown."

"Hey, Fillmore." I checked the rearview mirror, relieved to find him still considerably bleary-eyed.

"What's goin' on?"

"Almost there."

"It's dark."

"Fog's thick today."

"Um, kinda different. It doesn't look as built up."

"Drink this." He accepted the Bloody Mary bottle obediently. I watched him glug it down. "Yeah, slight detour. More construction around the airport."

He passed the bottle back. "Um, we're lucky, though. Not much traffic." He was squinting now, visually groping for anything familiar. I, of course, drove as quickly as possible to blur his chances of discovery. One particularly violent turn knocked him horizontal, and he was not to right himself again for some time.

THIRTY-ONE

The desert.

I traveled into blackness, the road making gentle turns, riding the bottom scrape of a vast, long-dead, primeval lake. No buildings, no cars. The radio signals had faltered in the wake of distant mountains, the only sound now an occasional tire bounce from below or snore from behind. The horizon stretched into stars. Barren, solemn miles occasionally broken by dark, unfamiliar shapes too remote to understand.

And then, rounding what seemed to be a swirl of sand dunes, my headlamps caught two men. Naked to the waist, they squatted, elbows on knees, wrists hanging limp, hunched over a small fire. One turned full-face into the oncoming cones of light, slack-jawed, protruding brow, primatial. I slowed the car, certainly more out of reflex and surprise than any desire to investigate.

Bare feet stamped out the flames, scuttled off into the night.

I was not quite certain what I'd seen, but since I felt responsible for the slumbering Fillmore, and was, after all, on an important assignment, I checked the door locks, rolled up the windows, and drove very fast indeed.

THIRTY-TWO

I saw the place long before I arrived. Most of the moon was out, and though the entry road banked and cambered, it afforded a clear line of sight miles into the canyon.

It was white, mainly, so it reflected the night sky and glowed a bit.

The main house was disturbingly left of center in a complicated complex of smaller outbuildings. Pointed arches and windows studded the facade of four levels that were heaped on one another like a hastily assembled wedding cake, the ground floor sporting a few additions where odd bulges had been attached in clumsy attempts at expansion.

There was little point in subterfuge. If Qina was in the house, she'd have picked up my headlights half an hour ago, so I pulled through the gates and parked.

I let myself out and had begun to examine the gargoyles when I heard a tiny, shaky piece of Fillmore's voice.

"Brown?"

A rear door opened, and he leveraged himself through. Staggering would not begin to describe it. Gasping would not begin to describe it. This was total, disoriented bewilderment. He had awoken in a moonscape as unlike Paris as it was possible to be.

For one low moment I toyed with the notion of pretending that this was Paris, such was the effect on me of the long drive, the desert stars, and the expression on Fillmore's face. But after all, enough is enough.

Fillmore's life had been thrown out of joint, his worldview rendered less reliable than a hologram. I placed a drumstick of capon in his right hand and poured out the last glass of Cabernet for the other.

He sank down in the sand, propped himself against a tire, and stared at Quilp's castle.

I kicked away a curious scorpion, strolled around a little, and gathered my powers of oration.

And I told him the story of the gas station sheriff in Furnace Flats, the Jeep Cherokee, the sombrero, the goggles, the Bloody Marys, and the likelihood that Qina was sequestered behind these very walls.

He seemed to take it all in with an admirable display of equanimity, the Valium no doubt still playing a considerable role. He requested more food.

I gave it, careful first to place the Armagnac in a most accessible position.

I walked around the car, whistling, pretending to absorb myself in the study of the entomological trophies stuck to my grille.

After several minutes of silent, meditative chewing, he got up, dusted himself off, and said, "Fifty-fifty."

"Pardon me?"

"Fifty-fifty, man. I'm here, you're here, fifty-fifty."

"You're referring to my fee."

"Correct."

"Ten percent."

"Hah!" Now he began to pace, counting out points of argument, one to a finger. "I'm not in Paris. I'm not on my way to Paris. I'm in Death Valley. I'm in Death Valley against my will. Oh God!" And here he stopped. "I'm in the middle of the hottest desert in the world without any sunblock."

"Twenty percent."

"I have extremely sensitive skin. It's two o'clock in the morning and I'm hot already."

"Twenty-five, my final offer."

"Fifty-fifty, man."

I sauntered up to the front door. "Well, if that's the way you feel, you can just wait out here by yourself."

"Thirty percent?"

"Done."

THIRTY-THREE

The front door was massive but such was the balance and precision of its hardware that it unlocked and swung open with all the resistance of cardboard. We were in the main hall, where, had we been so inclined, there was ample room for a vigorous game of tennis.

Ponderous leopard-skin chairs and zebra-striped sofas, broad slab-like tables, a wall of bleached, horned skulls, another of tribal masks, and a third of shells, teeth, dried tails, and porcupine quills—flagstones underneath.

Moonlight threw long shadows everywhere. Instinctively we were drawn to the fireplace opposite the door—an enormous cavity, big enough to have parked the Jeep inside. We traced a huge, stuffed snake up the sweep of chimney to the second-floor gallery where a large-bore, double-barrel shotgun pointed toward important areas of my chest.

THIRTY-FOUR

"Dr. Brown!"

"Yes," I said as brightly as possible, as though responding to a tap on my shoulder in the middle of a shopping mall on a Saturday afternoon. My ingenious delivery was undermined by Fillmore's loud and inartistic dive to shelter behind a nearby couch, but it produced the desired effect.

The voice was Qina's, and the click of her shotgun's safety mechanism echoed off the flagstones. She laid her rifle against the balustrade and Scarlet O'Haraed down the stairs into my arms.

"Oh, Dr. Brown." In the starlight she was nothing less than beautiful. She pressed, pulled us together. Her cheek, moistened with tears, warmed against my neck; her hips, as accurate as those of a First Avenue hooker, swayed below.

A perfect moment—actual clock time, perhaps one and a half seconds. Dr. Fillmore, having taken in the situation, was disinclined to play the role of "the other guy." He stood, knocking over an end table, and with it, a crystal decanter, six fluted glasses, and an ivory chess set.

"And...Dr. Fillmore?"

He was accorded the same reception, with, I was sorry to note, no reduction in pelvic intensity. After a time, she released him, stepped back between us. Her eyes narrowed, just, and a glint of hardness appeared. "How did you find me?"

Fillmore busied himself with broken glass, studied the chess set as though he'd never seen one before.

"We were just passing by and…" I groped for a punch line but surmised that this was not a good time for humor.

Qina's joints were loosening. She sagged a good two inches, rocked onto her heels. Steadying against the back of a couch she whispered, "My father."

Fillmore whipped around in panic. I nodded, delivered my line: "He's very concerned about you."

She made no reply, but continued to sag. First, down an arm of the sofa, then all but one leg over it onto the cushions.

Fillmore had by now separated out the unbroken goblets and discovered that the end table was also a liquor cabinet. He presented Qina a triple helping of brandy, inspected the label. "Germain Robin. This is what they serve in the White House."

I pretended to be very interested in the bottle, but watched her sideways. She did nothing. A coyote howled. Fillmore filled a couple more glasses and retreated into one of the leopard-skin chairs. I was feeling too guilty to move. The coyote howled again, louder now, or closer. Qina seemed to notice her drink for the first time, swallowed it all. She elbowed herself to a sitting position, held out her glass. I joined her on the couch, poured.

"You're working for my father."

"When I heard you were missing, I volunteered to find you." Fillmore and I avoided each other's eyes.

"How much is he paying you?"

"Well, he is picking up expenses. And paying me. But you see, he's very concerned about you."

"You said that."

"I think he'd like very much for you to come home."

"I'm sure of it." She finished drink number two. "Didn't I tell you he was going to kill Mother?"

"Well, not really. You said he was going to kill you."

"Of course I did, but I was pretending to be my mother."

"Right…why?"

"She was too scared to keep her appointment, to do anything, really. Especially after that incident with the crocodile."

"But you were the one with the scars."

Qina rubbed her thigh reflexively. "I was the one in the room."

"Your mother's room."

"Bedroom. I'd gone to borrow her car keys." She sighed slowly. "It was after lunch. On a typical day my mother would have gone in for a nap."

I'd seen Qina move enough to know she'd probably escaped on athletic ability alone. An older, drowsy mom would not have been so lucky. From Fillmore's corner: "And why do you believe your father would murder your mother?" The sort of question a therapist waits his whole career to ask.

"She had discovered he was the devil."

Fillmore. "Had discovered…?"

Qina watched his reaction. "The devil. I'd told Dr. Brown." As though this in some way supported the idea.

"Why didn't you ever mention that?" asked Fillmore.

"It seemed crazy."

Qina turned back to me. "Why do you think I came to see a psychologist?"

We all quietly played with our drinks. I suppose I hadn't mentioned this devil business to Fillmore because everything seemed somehow irrelevant once the patient was dead. But since we'd confirmed Qina was only a patient stand-in, the next question had to be, "Do you believe your father is the devil?"

I held my breath. If she answered yes, I could see enormous difficulties ahead. Father or not, Qina wasn't likely to allow herself to be willingly delivered to the devil. My fifty thousand dollars hung in the balance of her sanity.

"It's not like you think." Qina crossed the room, dragged a large, canvas carry-on bag out of the hall closet. She reached into an inner pocket, returned with a book. Dostoyevsky, *The Idiot*.

I cleared my throat at Fillmore, raised my eyebrows questioningly. He shook his head, shrugged his shoulders, and turned his palms to the ceiling.

Qina had her page marked, but she read as if she knew it by heart. "You laugh? You don't believe in the devil? Disbelief in the devil is a French idea, a frivolous idea. Do you know who the devil is? Do you know his name? Without even knowing his name, you laugh at the form of him…at his hoofs, at his tail, at his horns, which you have invented: for the evil spirit is a mighty, menacing spirit, but he has not the hoofs and horns you've invented for him."

I'd been examining my fingernails, looked up to discover Fillmore doing the same. But I knew I had him. Qina had possibly strayed into the region where a misstep by the therapist, however well intentioned, could cause problems worse than those the patient already suffered. And I was clearly out of my depth.

Fillmore shot me a murderous glance—I don't think the mention of anything "French" in Dostoyevsky's quote improved his disposition. But he was now in for thirty percent and made an attempt to be professional.

"What does that mean, exactly?"

Fillmore said this, but Qina spoke to me. "I just wanted to make sense of it. To get an outside perspective, to see if Mother…to see if we were getting it right." She grabbed my arm and squeezed— "To get help. The very idea was insane, so who do you tell? A shrink."

"I see." I needed to do that bit where I placed my fingertips together and nod wisely, but she still had a grip on my arm.

"Do you think I'm a lunatic?"

This was Fillmore's job now, but since she'd brought her face inches from mine, common courtesy demanded a reply.

"I…think…the death of a loved one is difficult. You're under a good deal of stress. It's understandable that delusions…"

"Delusions, huh?" She made another trip to the carry-on bag, returned with a mottled green *Reader's Digest*-sized pamphlet, all the way into my arms. "You dear, sweet man. I wonder if you're incapable of seeing evil in your fellow man."

"Me. Hah." But then again, never really thought about that one. Insanity, yes. Flawed characters, yes. Evil? I didn't know. Was that cretin in the pickup truck who cut me off on that exit ramp this afternoon evil?

"Dr. Brown?"

"Yes?" Qina was holding out the pamphlet for my inspection. A weapons manual, instructions for assembling a hand-held missile launcher, tips on maintenance, range-finding, and deployment.

"From a closet in my father's study. It was lying on top of the launcher itself. That was on top of a case of explosives, and that was on top of something else I couldn't identify."

If Quilp was a munitions dealer, it was no great surprise, none of my business, and for a man wealthy enough to know all the loopholes, probably not even illegal.

Not really the kind of stuff you leave hanging around the house, though.

Qina had taken possession of a rocking chair. It was the first time I could recall someone sitting in one without moving. She looked triumphantly at each of us in turn, her limbs rigid and locked, a glare in her eyes that flashed madness.

If she was fantasy-prone—and living in these houses how could she not be?—the impact of her mother's death could easily push her over the edge. She'd probably found the missile launcher book and confabulated the launcher itself.

"You probably think I just found this book and imagined I actually saw the weapons."

"Don't be ridiculous. But does it surprise you so much if your father deals in munitions? I understood he buys and sells anything."

"And," Fillmore put in, "that's hardly enough to qualify him as the...as a devil."

"Yes, I know, he's clever." Now she began to rock. "Last week a man came over to dine with my parents. Two nights later my mother and I saw his police mug shot on the evening news as the leader of the terrorist group that blew up the Beirut airport."

"How could she be sure it was the same man?"

"He had the same name."

"Your father…" began Fillmore.

"Is the devil." Saying it again suddenly seemed to give her peace.

She gathered herself up. "I fccl much better now. For the first time in days I think I can sleep. Please excuse me."

THIRTY-FIVE

"Disruption of serotonergic or noradrenergic forces influencing the neurochemical climate."

We were leaning against the Jeep, watching the sunrise, breakfasting on rum and mango juice. Qina had disappeared behind a door on the second floor. At first light, Fillmore had donned the sombrero, pocketed the goggles. He was now pacing and monologing.

"Have to take appropriate steps. Do we report this? If it's factual, the murder part, we're no longer doing therapy. We've got to weigh the safety concerns. But is it part of the fantasy?"

"It might just be theatrical."

"On both parts. Folie à deux, shared personality disorder."

"You think Quilp is trying to convince her he's the devil?"

"There's some primary process breaking through her surface. If she were a kid, I'd be thinking sexual molestation. Using the devil thing as a defense mechanism to cushion herself against reality. Pre-logical thinking."

"Primitive thinking." I had to hold up my end of the conversation.

"Yeah," said Fillmore, adjusting his chin strap. "The primitive mind is comfortable with familiar characters. That's why a kid can watch these mindless, repetitive Saturday morning cartoon shows. So, if she's reverted and living in a world of absolutes, blacks and whites, polar extremes…"

"She thinks bad Daddy killed good Mommy."

"And supplies terrorists, consorts with villains."

"She's Daddy's little girl again, but in this case, a daddy she hates and fears in the extreme."

"And who's the supreme bad guy?"

"Right. Got that. But she's not really in any danger, don't you think?"

"Help! Help! Aaaaahh!"

Qina. We ran for the house, with me in the lead, Fillmore having trouble getting traction in the sand, both of us careful not to spill our drinks.

"Aiahhh! Help! Dr. Brown!"

As I hit the first step, images of Qina in bed floated down to meet me. She was distressed, waking from a nightmare, face flushed, tearfully elegant, calling to me, needing comfort. Had she gone up to nap, loosening a few buttons, or was she undressed, sleeping in the nude? It would be the most natural thing to hold her, calm her, inform her that Fillmore was now her psychologist, lie next to her…

"Yaaah! Help!"

Having confidently assumed she was in the grip of some paranoid hypnopompic delusion, I was astonished to see her come tearing out her bedroom door, naked as I had hoped, but closely pursued by two men in dark uniforms. They sprinted the length of the hall, rounded a corner.

I had come full stop, maybe even taken a step backward. Fillmore had not. He plowed into me, spilling most of his drink down the back of my pants. I thought it best to finish what was left of mine and took up the chase.

They had a sizable lead, and we tracked them on noise alone. Qina was fast—I think anyone naked can always run a bit faster—and we all raced through the house at a good clip. Up stairs, down stairs, through the kitchen, the dining room, the library, the billiard room, another dining room, the sauna, the servants' quarters, around the garage, back into the main hall, up the main staircase.

We caught sight of them once, watching from above as they ran across the courtyard. Qina had stretched out a lead of several furlongs.

"Fillmore! Let's split up. I'll go this way."

"Wait a second, man. I don't want to run into those two guys by myself."

I actually hadn't given much thought to what we might do if we ever caught up. There had been something on one of the corridor walls that looked like a war club, and I went back for it.

It was around this time I noticed that Fillmore was taking great pains to ensure I was always in the lead. This could be a valuable piece of guilt to throw at him if he ever wanted to negotiate up from his thirty percent.

The noise of a powerful engine catching hold. We rushed out to the driveway in time to watch Qina power-shift into second gear, roaring and squealing into the canyon behind the wheel of a midnight blue Lotus Super Seven. A second roar, muffled with a hint of whine, as a black Jaguar sedan fishtailed in pursuit.

"Fillmore, come on!" A selection awaited in the garage, all keyed and polished. There was an Aston Martin I would have liked and a Porsche speedster I'd look great in, but the closest was a dirt bike, one of those red Japanese things with oversize tires.

"Yes, Fillmore. Hop on. Let's go!"

Great moments can sometimes foster great mistakes. I can see now the suggestion that Fillmore take the back seat was one of these. Costumed for battle in his sombrero and goggles, brandishing the war club, he did, though, seem a man of destiny.

We came around the house and down the drive at maximum acceleration, the speed and centrifugal force conspiring to push us a few inches off the pavement. It was enough. The knobby miracle tires hit the sand and dug in for the day.

Fillmore shook his fist, growled like a caveman, and fell backward off the bike. We listened to the sounds of our quarry fade down the canyon walls for a while and then trudged back to the house. This time we played it safe, taking the Jeep. Fillmore thought to raid the Quilp liquor cabinet, extracting a few particularly expensive selections, and we were off again, in a very distant third place.

My fifty thousand dollars, which Fillmore had whittled down to thirty-five, was now naked and insane, bolting through Death Valley, California, with two thugs in hot pursuit.

THIRTY-SIX

There was only one road in and out of the canyon, and I was surprised to see another car coming toward us. A police car. He switched on his flashers and stopped at an angle that blocked our way.

We waited while he took his time walking to us. A tall, skinny man with a potbelly, he was dressed in grimy khakis, sunglasses, a wide-brimmed forest ranger hat, and he carried a rifle.

"Hello, boys. Mind if I see your driver's license and some registration?" He peered through my window across at Fillmore, who, frozen in the moment, was still in costume.

"Is there some problem, Officer?"

"Well, you know, this being private property, I was wondering what you fellas were doing here." He fingered my license and studied Fillmore fumbling in the glove compartment. I joined the search, console, door pockets, behind the visor. There were no registration papers.

"We're guests of Mr. Quilp, the owner. I'm sorry about the registration, but this is a new car and…"

"Do you have some identification, Pancho?" This to Fillmore, who produced his driver's license. We watched glumly as the officer lined it up with mine and buttoned both in his shirt pocket. "Now, can you fellas just turn around, and I'll follow you on up to the house."

THIRTY-SEVEN

Our chase had, of course, left the place in chaos. To compound matters, the bottles Fillmore liberated bore Quilp's private stamp on the label. The protests and pleas that Sheriff Mike, our new acquaintance, call Quilp had to wait until we arrived at the place we now sat, Furnace Flats Jail. Suspicion of car theft, breaking and entering.

Ninety-three degrees and climbing, no clouds. The walls were gray, the mattress on which we both sat was gray, and the huge raven perched between the bars of our only window was black. There was a cement partition across from our cell, which blocked not only our view of the sheriff's office, but also any breeze that might wander through.

Sheriff Mike had phoned Quilp, who was unavailable, as was Ms. Adrian.

"Guess this means you fellas are gonna be guests of the county awhile."

"Wait. Can you call Stanford University? I'm on the faculty. I'm sure they'll be able to…" Fillmore by now looked like many things, none of which was a college professor.

"I'm sure they might," returned the sheriff, as though arresting Stanford faculty was a tiresome part of his daily routine, "but just 'cause somebody knows who you are don't excuse no crime. Now, this'll have to hold you till I get back."

Sheriff Mike passed in a jar of water, already lukewarm, a plate of biscuits, and the morning paper. He apparently had not heard Fillmore's request for a pillow.

I borrowed the sombrero and goggles—Fillmore looked somehow incomplete without them—and slept.

THIRTY-EIGHT

No feeling in my shoulder, no ignoring the heat. Three o'clock by Fillmore's watch. He'd certainly slept sufficiently the day before, but looked to have napped off most the afternoon for lack of other options. I watched a small horned lizard cross a Fillmore shoe, pause motionless on the open newspaper beneath my shadow, and dart out of sight as I pushed myself upright.

The sports section, front page. On a particularly bad day, in a hot, hungover moment in the Death Valley jail from which I would have thought it possible to sink no lower, I descended.

"GAMBLING CHAMP DETHRONED. Backgammon Upset of the Decade."

My state of mind was such that instead of merely picking up the pages, I fell to my knees to read.

"Easy Money, legendary Las Vegas sportsman, last month's winner of the Hong Kong International and holder two years running of the prestigious London Invitational Backgammon Cup, was beaten in a challenge match at San Francisco's Fairmont Hotel by Ms. Rebecca Sue Siegelman, a reporter for the *Boston Examiner*."

A befuddled Rebecca, squinting at the flashbulbs, her one good arm raising the neck of an enormous trophy, supported by a suspiciously gracious Easy Money.

"Ms. Siegelman, who later confessed her experience was limited to a few childhood matches at the Brentwood Country Club in Great Neck, New York, appeared at first to have not realized she'd won.

"'I wasn't really sure the game was over,' said the bewildered Ms. Siegelman. 'I didn't have time to learn all the rules.'"

Had I not been so depleted, so hot; had I guessed, as I was later to learn, that Easy Money had manipulated Rebecca's victory in order to win a far larger bet against himself, I probably would not have screamed.

Fillmore shot to his feet, gawked around wildly, and a voice said, "It's all right, men. Buck up. I'm on the job. Don't worry about a thing."

We both looked through the bars of our window, a full ten feet off the ground, at a smiling face, which I noticed without surprise was that of Mr. Casbarian.

He drew a heavy rope around the bars and disappeared. Seconds later the rope tensed, twanged, and we heard a shower of fine concrete pebbles hit the ground outside, followed by, "Again, King! Giddyap! Giddyap, Rambo!" A second shower, heavier. Cracks appeared in our wall.

I made myself comfortable on the floor. "Fillmore."

"Yes!" Impatiently. "What?"

"Mr. Casbarian's here."

"Pull, Rambo! Pull, Norman! On, King!"

The jail snapped in protest, but its ancient angles began to sag hopelessly against the will of Mr. Casbarian.

"Giddyap! Charge! Charge!"

Each bar had been sunk a good two feet above and four feet below the window frame. When they burst free, most of the wall toppled in their wake.

The dust cleared to reveal Mr. Casbarian astride a golden palomino stallion, freeing his towrope from a matched set of pintos.

Fillmore was the first to move. "Mr. Casbarian. What are you doing?"

"Hurry, Dr. Fillmore." He handed down a set of reins.

"But, Mr. Casbarian, we're in no danger. We've done nothing wrong."

Mr. Casbarian could have been created nowhere but Hollywood, but to his credit, it must be said that he created himself.

He spurred his mount inside, presented me "Rambo!" with a wink.

Sometimes it's best simply to yield to the demands of an overwhelming personality. And there was no defending oneself against a Mr. Casbarian.

"I had to see you, Dr. Brown. I apologize for being early for our next appointment, but I think I've had a break-through."

Fillmore was in semi-shock, but struggled obediently onto Norman. "Christ! All right, man. Let's get out of here."

But Mr. Casbarian had now slipped into a particularly captivating memory. "You know, boys, I can remember a similar experience. In the Sudan. Oh, gee, I guess now that must be a good fifteen, twenty years ago. Anyway, desert much like this. Horses there a bit more of a rarity, though.

Well, it seems one of my mates had gotten into a brouhaha with some local chief over…"

"Mr. Casbarian!" Fillmore was having trouble on the overeager Norman, who spun continually in his excitement.

"Yes. Quite right, Doctor." Mr. Casbarian rode alongside the rapidly paling Fillmore, stopped Norman with a sharp pull on his bridle. I swung onto Rambo. Mr. Casbarian balanced his weight over King's and saddle horn, pivoted left, pivoted right, and shaded his eyes into the afternoon sun.

"Now, men, let's ride!" And we galloped into the Valley of Death.

THIRTY-NINE

Ten minutes later we cantered up the driveway of the Desert Sands Spa. There had been an open stretch of gravel-tanned mesa, then a smooth, white swirl of dunes rippling to the edge of a steep, jagged mountain, and around the corner, U.S. Highway 190.

"Mr. Casbarian." Fillmore's voice was one part aggravation, nine parts resignation. "What's going on?"

"Mr. Casbarian!" The doorman jumped to attention. Two of them actually, gotten up as officers in the dress uniform of some mythical cowboy militia—loops of gold braids through the epaulets of Western-style tunics, wide-brimmed ten-gallon hats studded and dangled with stars, delicate hand-tooled boots wrapped over striped, balloon-style riding pants.

They rushed to attend his dismount. "How was it, sir?"

"Exhilarating. Just the thing." He sprang to the ground, waved grandly in our direction. "My guests. Dr. Brown, Dr. Fillmore."

I did my best to imitate the Casbarian dismount. The doormen eyed Fillmore nervously but in the end were able to reunite him and the earth with a minimum of uniform mangling and toe crushing.

"Follow me, Doctors." Mr. Casbarian stuffed his riding gloves in a back pocket and led us through the air-conditioned lobby, up a broad staircase to a set of golden doors marked Sagebrush Suite. Inside, a tall man absentmindedly swirled ice inside a half-full cocktail glass; another spoke in hushed tones on a cattle-horned telephone.

The tall man grinned. "Mr. Casbarian." And to us, "Gentlemen." He reached for a frosted pitcher. "I took the liberty of mixing refreshments in anticipation of your arrival."

We three accepted long, iced glasses of something orange floated with a red liqueur and tasting vaguely of bourbon. We four sat. The telephone man consulted a thick address book, made another call.

"Everything go all right?" asked our host.

"Yes, fine. Fun." Mr. Casbarian took a measured sip. "I'm sorry. My manners. Dr. Brown, Dr. Fillmore...Governor Hershon."

I thought that guy had looked familiar.

"My pleasure, gentlemen. Any friends of Mr. Casbarian..."

Mr. Casbarian raised his glass in affirmation.

I have always excelled in situations where doing nothing was both the proper and the prudent course. When waiters arrived with room service, I accepted it as my due, surveyed the laying out of plates with a critical eye; let the air-conditioning seep deeply through my clothing; relaxed, knowing that it would only be seconds before Fillmore...

"Mr. Casbarian! What…you knocked down the jail! Sorry," (a hidden finger pointing in the governor's direction) "he knows that, right?"

The governor took his place at the table. "Mr. Casbarian has this morning made a more than generous donation toward the building of a new, sorely needed, modern sheriff's office for this too often neglected part of the state."

Fillmore's nose found itself drawn to the garlic-laced trails of fire-roasted scampi. "But…umhhhh…but how did you…?"

"CLETS. California Law Enforcement Teletype Service." Mr. Casbarian seated himself at the head of the table. "I keep a terminal in my condo, always run through the morning action. When your names popped up, I thought it might be fun to invite Marc, Governor Hershon, on a little vacation. And"—he raised his eyebrows sheepishly at me—"hopefully work in a session?"

Mr. Casbarian fixed a plate of prosciutto and melon, pointed it questioningly in my direction, and placed it in front of the chair to his right. "You two have rooms down the hall." He checked his watch. "Now, we're all scheduled for herbal wraps and a massage in forty-five minutes, so *bon appetite*."

FORTY

"No, Doctor." Mr. Casbarian was pacing. "Ah, it's common enough, but so innocently, unconsciously death-defying. Never. Never. Underestimate the desert."

I grabbed the champagne from the ice bucket, emptied most of what remained into a silver cup with the face of a steer, horns for handles.

"Southern Algeria. Professor Lane and a geologist named Goldberg. Experienced, made the trip a dozen times. Possibly ten kilometers camp to camp, but they were overtaken by a sandstorm and panicked. We managed to find them two days later, one hundred and seven miles off course."

Mr. Casbarian folded his arms with the satisfaction of a story well told. Thus far our entire "session" had consisted of Mr. Casbarian educating me on the finer points of desert survival. I now knew three ways to rig a compass, two time-proven methods for catching the eyes of search plane pilots, and in a slight departure from normal psychiatric approach, watched a brief demonstration in the parking lot on how to fashion slip-noose snares out of engine wires.

"Great stuff, Mr. Casbarian. Fascinating. But I'm afraid our time is up now. I do want to thank you again for a terrific dinner."

"Oh. Time's up? Hmh. You're…ah…"

"Yes, pretty tired."

"I understand." He stopped at the door. "Not all that far from Las Vegas…"

Tempted, but temptation tempered by the news of the Rebecca–Easy Money affair. "No, a long day for me."

"You and Dr. Fillmore will accompany us in the governor's jet back to San Francisco in the morning? I'll arrange for a man to drive your Jeep back tonight."

I spread my arms magnanimously. "Why not?"

FORTY-ONE

I could not remember the last time I wore pajamas. Childhood. But Mr. Casbarian had sent a bellboy up with a soft, silken pair bearing the Desert Sands Spa crest, a bottle of Martell Cordon Bleu, and a copy of *Modern Man in the Primitive World, Volume VI—Poisons and Hallucinogens, Rites of Passage, Tribal Warfare (Nomads)*.

A knock, Fillmore let himself through the door adjoining our suites. Matching pajamas. He held up *Volume IX—Headhunting*. "You get one of these?"

"Yes. Do you figure he always travels with stuff like this?"

"Who can guess anything about Mr. Casbarian?" This from a psychologist.

We were both, however, coming off several hours of pampering and, at bottom, unwilling to make too many jokes at Mr. Casbarian's expense.

The door to the hallway began to scratch and rattle, eventually emerging as a timid knock. Fillmore had been approaching the cognac, but now took a measured step backward. "Your room, man."

I opened the door onto Sheriff Mike, hat in hand, pawing, toeing the rug with a boot. "Hi."

"Hi."

"Hi."

Fillmore and I in identical striped pajamas, Sheriff Mike seemingly unable to move.

"Everything all right, Sheriff?"

He swallowed, let himself in. "You…fellas…psychiatry men. That right?"

Neither Fillmore nor I wanted to field that one, but Sheriff Mike appeared willing to wait indefinitely.

"Yes."

"I…" He caught sight of the book title in Fillmore's hand, lost the predicate of his sentence.

"Yes, Sheriff, you…?"

"I…"

"Please, Sheriff, sit down," said Fillmore, retreating to his own quarters, sliding the door lock into place.

"Sorry about all that. You know, today, all that stuff."

"Ah, don't worry, Sheriff. I totally understand. You can go to sleep with a clear conscience."

"No."

"No?"

"No, see, I don't sleep none too well. It's not a mind thing or nothing, this pain I get. A coupla the boys over by the Dusty Door think maybe so, but I know different."

"A mind thing?"

"Yeah, it's not that."

"What isn't?"

"This transmitter."

"What transmitter?"

"From the army. They implanted some transmitter in my brain. It's always vibratin'." He grabbed his temples in proof.

"Vibrating? Well, that's nothing. Just think of it as a massage. It'll put you right to sleep." I put my hand reassuringly on his shoulder, tried to lift him by the arm. "Good night, Sheriff Mike."

"When they activate it, that's when it hurts. Some kinda radar. Hardens up everything in my nose like rocks. Gives me dandruff. I think stuff comes out of my ears, too."

"Maybe if you tried a little soap in there..." I had him standing now, but I couldn't get him moving.

"They can't control me anymore, though. I'm too strong. I got the power."

"You do."

"Yes." He tightened his lips into a thin smile, looked me in the eyes for the first time. "Psychic power. Like to help the police find something."

"Like what?"

"Don't know. There's never anything missing around here. Sometime I'll just wander around that desert for days, looking for stuff."

He sat again. "I think it started back at Fort Polk. That's Louisiana. Never did see any combat. I was an MP, stateside. Yeah...so, anyhow, one night...sit down, Doctor, this won't take too long. One night...well, come to think of it, maybe this started when I was little. See, I grew up in this shitass, nothing town in Texas. I guess as a kid I never had..."

FORTY-TWO

Not sure how much sleep I really got. I woke in a chair at sunrise to Sheriff Mike pumping my hand, thanking me, apologizing again for the arrest, thanking me again, and then, thankfully, leaving.

Fillmore and I wound up as the only passengers on the state of California's premier jet. Mr. Casbarian had decamped to Las Vegas, the governor and staff to the Cellular Phone Festival in Malibu.

"Now, obviously, Quilp uses his wealth as an all-purpose tool." Fillmore paused as I discovered the governor's private cache of cigars. We lit up, and he continued on the exhale. "He even uses it psychologically. His method, his remedy for resolving inner conflicts, which, in this instance, includes working through family problems...I bet these are Cuban cigars, man."

We each pocketed an assortment.

"So," Fillmore went on, "as to your case. Quilp has a problem with his daughter; he simply hires someone to make it better. Now what we have to tell him," he pointed his cigar, "what you have to tell him."

"We."

"OK, you with me maybe helping a little bit."

"Thirty percent."

"Right, thirty percent. Anyway, let's see…we'll just say she seems to have a rich fantasy life."

"That I can do. But don't mention the devil thing?"

"Well, without the patient around it's hard to explore the extent to which her delusion system is fixed."

"You mean, as long as I'm coming back empty-handed, no sense upsetting Quilp more than we have to."

"Exactly, man. We will say…" and here a couple of slow puffs to aid thought, "that…we are developing hypotheses related to the possibility of thought disorders relative to delusions, relative to her reality contact."

"You better say that."

"Then what's left for you to say?"

"I'll ask if she ever claims to hear voices."

"Not enough."

"OK. I'll ask about voices and hallucinations."

"No," said Fillmore, "if I'm going to stick around on this, man, you have to ask about voices and hallucinations and… about those two guys."

FORTY-THREE

I was alone. Fillmore had called his service, acted over-flustered over some unnamed, minor emergency, and split. "Gotta split, man."

All right. I'd beaten the Jeep back to town, and even though I felt no immediate, pressing need for transportation, decided it was probably time to retrieve my Healey from the Larkspur ferry parking lot.

Taxi to the Embarcadero. Took a hot dog, root beer, and chocolate chip cookie to the dock and watched my ship come in.

It was a good day to be on the water. Light chop, few clouds. I carried a martini to the stern, choosing a seat directly over the engine where the fumes never failed to remind me of those puttering launches that shuttle about the Greek Islands.

The weather on the Marin side of the bay was perfect as always. Sunlight sparkled off the dents in my hood, bounced dazzlingly around the remaining struts of my grille.

Two spiders fought for strategic web position on the steering wheel. Otherwise, everything pretty much OK.

What the hell? As long as I was this close I figured I might as well stop off at Quilp's.

Across and through Larkspur Landing to 101, south a couple of exits to Mill Valley. Brightly dressed, fifteen-speed cyclists absentmindedly swerving into traffic; pony-tailed strolling guitarists absentmindedly jaywalking into traffic; BMWs cheek to jowl with mud-caked pickup trucks; hippies and yuppies locked in irresolute struggle for dominance.

Deep into the canyon a bearded man balanced a typewriter against the railing of a rough, redwood deck; a yellow pencil behind his ear, a drink raised in smiling acknowledgment of my passing down this quiet road. Summer-tanned women, brows tensed, T-shirts moistened, jogged by in weightless, pastel underwear. Golden retrievers, Irish setters, and a solitary pug bounced in happy accompaniment.

Quilp Valley Road. Back through the old stone fence, second gear straining against the angle of ascent. A few twists and turns and a huge truck blocking the way. No driver, apparently no one in shouting distance.

There was a cutoff veering left, so I took it.

The redwoods gave way to another kind of tree I couldn't identify. No leaves, just black branches that threw off undulating, serpentine shadows when stirred by the breeze. The fog came in suddenly, tight and thick, rushing off the Pacific toward the San Joaquin Valley.

Cooler now, and darker. The breeze became a wind, cracking and popping the limbs overhead.

The road curved right, paralleling the main drive. An occasional trash barrel or shed made it a service road. The smell was of fresh meat, and under that, a strong musk, and I knew the animal cages must be nearby.

117

The house lay ahead, shielded by a carefully clipped hedge that rimmed a small sunken parking lot. A loading dock, a dumpster, and a truck jammed with gardening tools. There was no way to pull around to the front, but the hedge itself was incised with onion-shaped entries of varying height. I parked near the largest, walked through into a formal garden.

It wasn't a labyrinth, but it had that feel. Fountains, bushes, statuary—everything so unreasonably overdone, so massive, that there was no clear line of sight for more than a few yards in any direction. I took what seemed to be the most logical turnings and wound up at the edge of a courtyard across from a two-story wall of windows.

These were the old-fashioned kind, wooden framed, each pane not much larger than the palm of my hand.

But inside, an immense chandelier was blazing, as well as rows of lustrous track lights studded around the perimeter, and it was not difficult to see everything going on.

Only one thing, however, was going on. Quilp was sitting on a thin, high-back chair, naked; and equally unclothed and dangling from the ceiling in a harness made of leather and possibly green fleece, was Ann Adrian. Her body arched and strained, breasts bulging painfully against the restraints. Arms and legs swung free but for thick cuffs leashed to her wrists and ankles, another buckled at the neck. Muscles in her shoulders and thighs shivered with intensity. There were straps on Quilp's legs, the contraption rigged so that he could control Ann Adrian's vertical motion by opening and closing his knees. She was now between them, her head rising and falling in delighted screams and muffled gasps in response to Quilp's pulsations.

Suffice it to say that the idea of kissing Ann Adrian would never be the same.

But the shock of carnality, the erotic surrendering, the raw force of Quilp's sexual appetite, momentarily fixed me to the spot. And in that moment, Quilp turned around.

The pitch of bestial power in the room never lessened, but for just a couple of seconds it seemed Quilp caught me, visually, over one shoulder and grinned.

Now, all odds against this were in my favor. The sunlight was slanting between drifts of fog directly into his eyes, the room lights themselves were on, I was mostly in shadow, still at the far side of the courtyard, motionless, and certainly unannounced and unexpected. But this almost rabid, triumphant smile came right at me. Both his eyes and lips were stretched, his brows unnaturally high, his neck twisted well beyond the comfort range.

I retreated into the garden, doubled back toward my car, and immediately became lost. I panicked, ran around in circles for a few minutes, fully expecting Quilp to pounce at me from every conceivable place of hiding, calmed myself by considering what Mr. Casbarian might do in such a spot, and made my way coolly to the parking lot.

I put the Healey in neutral, pushed it until I used up most of my adrenaline, and climbed in. I had my fingers on the key, poised over the ignition. In the rearview mirror, an old man. He was thirty or forty feet away, but he knew I'd seen him. I turned around. The man was gray-haired with a gray beard, and as he went for the trees I could see a pair of binoculars swinging from his neck.

Quilp's security force? No, why would he run for cover? If part of his job was not to be noticed? But why hire an old man for skulking around in the woods?

I was moving now, but I was, in a sense, stuck. Seen, I'd have to continue on up to the house.

When I reached the turnoff to the main drive, the truck was conveniently absent. I slowed, stalling for time. If I could partially exorcise my memories of Quilp, Ann Adrian, and the harness, or at least shove them back into a seldom-visited section of my brain, I might pull this off all right.

I tried to concentrate on sports, which worked a bit; then that led to thoughts of Rebecca and her victorious, front-page headlines, which, though painful, worked even better.

Thus it was that I pulled up to Daniel Quilp's mansion a second time. Nonchalantly twirling the Austin Healey keys around my index finger, I made my way to his front doors.

The underbelly of the fog had stiffened with deep blues and grays. It grew dark, the shadows disappeared. I rang the bell and waited. There wasn't much to do on the porch, so I began to examine the carved autographs that I'd earlier mistaken for some bizarre design. The elements had blurred and softened a lot of them, but there was one, rather large and crudely done, close to the left door latch that looked for all the world like A-d-o-l-f H-i-t-l-e-r. A closer inspection revealed nothing to dispel this impression.

It seemed everybody I was dealing with lately turned out to be somehow crazy.

Was this what people meant by "California"?

"Dr. Brown."

"What?…Oh, Ms. Adolph, uh, Ms. Adrian. Hello."

She was dressed, unwrinkled, but breathing a little hard. "Very nice of you to stop by. Please, come in."

I followed her through the foyer, down a stairway, then down another into a trophy room, smaller, but not unlike the one I'd left behind in Death Valley. Outraged predators, ten heads to a wall, eyes wide, gums bared, teeth sharpened. The taxidermist had gone for menace, but underneath that, each conveyed a sort of suspended bewilderment, deprived of body and limb, a sense that something had gone horribly wrong.

Two rings, Ann Adrian picked up a telephone, offered me an arched eyebrow and part of a smile.

"Mr. Quilp will receive you in the study."

Midway down another flight of stairs. "Most of the rooms are underground here. We have guest quarters on the level after this if you'd care to spend the night."

Right.

Quilp had taken less pains with his attire than had Ms. Adrian. He'd thrown on a ridiculous red silk smoking jacket, pants to match. He was, however, smoking.

"Dr. Brown." Quilp waved me to a chair. Opening a large folder, he leaned into the corner of a sharp-edged Oriental desk and proceeded to ignore me for ten minutes.

Something amusing on the last page. He chuckled to himself and flipped the folder over his head.

I had by now succumbed to the effects of being subterranean and was scaring myself with fantasies having to do with the full weight of these many stories crushing through the ceiling.

Quilp proclaimed, "Cocktails," and crossed to the far side of the room where a large, black marble wet bar hummed in refrigerated repose. His position at the desk had effectively blocked from view the wall behind.

That, along with the fact that I had been reluctant to look in his direction, meant that I now had my first clear look at the decorations in front of me.

Pictures of the presidents of the of the United States, but each one somehow bizarre and all of them new to me. There was a photograph of Woodrow Wilson taken, apparently, after a bad fall. One of Kennedy with a bandaged eye, Eisenhower removing something from his shoe, Franklin Roosevelt in the hospital, Teddy Roosevelt in poorly fitting underwear, Warren Harding staring curiously at his crotch, and George Bush smelling something bad. The set was complete back to George Washington with the earlier presidents represented in caricature of the period.

Free from photographic reality, these were brutal—the audience clapping at Lincoln's assassination, Andrew Jackson in full retreat, Ulysses S. Grant as a hopeless, slobbering drunk, Thomas Jefferson chained to a toilet, Millard Fillmore in tears.

"Dr. Brown." It was cognac for me and another of those green potions for Quilp. He seated himself at the desk directly beneath a blowup of Herbert Hoover squeezing a pimple.

"Thank you." I raised my glass. "Here's to…"

"What have you been doing?"

"I?"

"Yes. Your shoes look muddy."

"Oh, my car leaks."

"I see. Not in our Jeep, then."

"No. About the Jeep, actually. I'd like to ask…"

"I'm aware of the entire affair. Sheriff Mike eventually got through to me. Very sorry about the absence of papers, but I didn't know Ms. Adrian had given you the car. You see, I thought you were in Paris."

"No, no, I…"

"Tell me about my daughter. I understand you weren't able to retrieve her, but how was she when you last saw her?"

"To tell you the truth, there were these two men…"

"Yes, they work for me."

"Ahhh." I thought it best to pretend to be holding my own. Unable to follow "Ahhh" with another sentence, however, I remained on much the lighter side of the scales.

"I hope you don't think it unreasonable that I'd put some of my own people on an important problem. The main thing is to get Qina back."

This news cut both ways. If those were Quilp's men, I probably didn't have to worry about them breaking an assortment of bones in my body if we again crossed paths.

But it also seemed that I now had rivals for the fifty thousand dollars I'd begun, almost paternally, to consider my own. Come to think of it, if Quilp had offered these guys the same financial incentive, they probably wouldn't hesitate to smash anyone in their way.

"Now, about Qina."

"Qina, well, the last time I saw her she was driving away in a blue Lotus Seven, chased by your men." My tone conveyed unbridled contempt at the idea that anyone but myself was suitable for this particularly delicate pursuit.

"She eluded them." Quilp lifted his chin, pursed his lips, and poured down his drink, all in about three seconds.

"Qina," he went on, "was schooled in the intricacies of high performance at Scars Point." He then laughed his piercing poodle laugh, loudly, standing to do so. I was so shocked I rose with him.

Quilp looked at me in much the same way he had through the courtyard windows minutes before, and took his seat. "Sit down, Dr. Brown."

I, standing foolishly to no purpose, saved the moment, boldly reaching for his glass. "Can I get you a refill?"

"Yes," he said, punctuated with a single, slow nod.

I selected Léopold Gourmel for myself, a cognac recently risen so sharply in price that I'd had to cut it from my shopping list. Quilp's green stuff was in a silver and glass decanter. It poured like the last cup of coffee from the urn. We tilted our goblets to each other with gentlemanly good grace, and I sat.

"Qina," he said.

"Yes, your daughter…is fine, pretty much. She…you were right, she took your wife's death hard, and…"

"You spoke with her for some time?"

"Yes. Yes, I did."

"Why won't she return home?"

"She…ah…was she on any medication or anything?"

"Not that I'm aware of. What are you getting at?"

"No medication. Um, well, she was kind of acting strangely." What was it Fillmore had said? A rich fantasy life? "She seems to have a rich fantasy life."

"Are you saying my daughter is having fantasies caused by drugs?"

"No, no."

"An undigested bit of beef, perhaps?"

"No."

"Well, you're a psychologist, what are you trying to tell me?"

I should have foreseen this turn the conversation was taking. The appealing notion that I could just pop in on one of the wealthiest men in the world had blurred the likely consequences. Undone, once again, by my own vanities.

"Dr. Brown?"

I should have memorized that double-talk about hypotheses relative to hallucinations relative to reality relative to…

"Dr. Brown?"

"Right, uh, has she ever acted like this before?"

"Run away, no."

"She never seemed disturbed or…?"

I'd pressed the button I'd tried hardest to avoid. Quilp jumped up from his seat and screamed, "Mental illness does not run in my family!"

How had I let myself get trapped into playing psychologist again? Now one of the wealthiest men in the world was furious at me. I wasn't quite sure this was Fillmore's fault, but since he was in for thirty percent, I decided to suggest Quilp call him.

I was about to confess that I was in over my head as a mental health practitioner, confident that I could pull that off without relinquishing my role as private investigator, when we were joined by Ann Adrian. She handed us each a towel and opened a thin black door next to a photo of Lyndon Johnson pretending to pick up his wife by the ears.

Quilp's eyes had glazed over some. He seemed to be absorbed with concerns other than those in the room, but a small voice came out of the corner of his mouth: "Steam up?"

"Yes, Mr. Quilp."

He refocused on me. "I trust, Dr. Brown, as a key man in my employ, that you are not merely lowering your own levels of stress by attempting to take cognitive control of our situation. Come."

Ann Adrian took my hand, and we followed Quilp through the doorway into a corridor of dark red tiles. We took a turn and stepped into a semicircular room with wooden benches and a crude wooden door.

She unbuttoned my shirt, motioned for me to sit down, and took off my shoes and socks. I was still a little disconcerted—no one but my editors and my old girlfriend had yelled at me in years—so I accepted this enforced disrobing without sufficient question. Quilp had stripped down and wrapped the towel around his waist. We were meant to take a steam bath together. I didn't want to, moved to whisper as much to the closest thing I had to an ally in the room, Ms. Adrian, but she had disappeared.

The wooden door opened with a burst of smoke. A small but solidly built woman emerged. She had straight blond hair and a sleeveless pink terrycloth robe that unerringly matched the superheated flush of her arms and legs.

"This is Einstein. Einstein, the eminent Dr. Brown." Quilp mistook my reluctance for shyness. "Come on, Brown. We're in Marin County. Now put on your towel and get over here."

Half-undressed and only steps away from the steam room, I was socially cornered. The two watched as I began to take off my pants, and, satisfied, they slipped behind the wooden door.

FORTY-FOUR

My towel was an inch too short. I held my breath and managed a tiny knot over one hip, but it sprang loose. I could just hold the two ends with my thumb and finger, and doing so, walked into the mist.

I could see nothing. Worse, I suddenly remembered I hate steam baths. Too humid.

"Over here."

I groped around blindly, my one free hand waving protectively in front of my face, and slapped Quilp across his right cheek.

"Sorry."

I thought I heard Einstein muffle a giggle, but it could have been the hissing of the steam. Quilp muttered to himself and lay back. Einstein arranged towels to help him stretch out facedown, then took off the pink robe and straddled his hips. As she began to massage his shoulders, I backed away and fell onto a bench. I was already hotter than I cared to be.

"I find it difficult to relax," strained Quilp in high, cracked syllables. "This helps."

"Nothing like a steam bath," I returned stupidly.

"Now, you haven't given me an answer. Why won't my daughter come home?"

The vapors had already made me a little light-headed, the cognac a little bold, so I risked it.

"She seems to be afraid."

"Of what?"

"Well, uh, you."

"Me?" Even though he tried to hold his voice in check, "me" was drawn out for several seconds, ending in a long, quivering growl. "Why?"

"I guess she holds you responsible in some way for your wife's death."

"What you psychologists might call projection."

"Uh, well…"

"Come now, she can avoid feeling bad herself by placing the onus on others."

"Yes, that's it more or less."

"Hmm."

I couldn't see either of them clearly, but flashes of Einstein occasionally appeared in the fog. She made her way rhythmically up and down Quilp's spine, that most private part of her brushing off the small of his back as she writhed into each thrust.

"Why would Qina think I killed her mother?"

"No, I don't think she thinks that you actually…"

"Did she tell you I was the devil?"

"Uh, yes, she did say something like that."

"I see."

Einstein tossed a dipper of cold water in my face, one for Quilp, then herself.

Quilp appeared to have risen onto his elbows. "You asked me if I thought I could ascribe pathology to my wife's side of the family." A good question, but I'd never asked it. "I think so. You see, my wife was involved with...the occult. Heavily, too heavily, I suppose. It seems now that she had entangled Qina to a far greater extent than I'd feared."

"I see."

"Do you? Good. I actually abhor the storytelling myths of classic psychology, but in every age both the disorder and the cure fit the times."

Einstein mumbled her assent.

"Beyond that," Quilp went on, "certain patterns are resistant to change because they're self-rewarding. This blaming the devil for your troubles would seem to be the most enduring. And in this age, our New Age, how large a step, really, from belief in astrology, psychic surgery, UFO abductions, spoon bending, crystal healing, and trance channeling to belief in the devil incarnate?"

This might be true, but if there were a devil, I certainly wouldn't put it past him to have invented all those other things.

Quilp paused to flip onto his back, rotating his hips between Einstein's thighs. He laced both hands behind his head and the massage continued, emphasized now with yelps—though it was difficult to make out from whom.

"I'm, whew, that's about all for me. Hot. I'll just head for the showers."

No response. I shuffled slowly in the general direction of the door, looking for all the world like a blind, one-armed beggar I'd once seen in Calcutta. Unfortunately, not only had the heat affected my sense of direction, but I had no way of knowing the size and shape of the room. When I finally found the exit, many minutes had gone by, and Quilp and Einstein were right behind me.

Quilp studied me curiously. He could easily assume I'd been voyeuring behind the steam, and if he had earlier seen me through the courtyard windows, that meant, from his point of view, the second time in less than an hour.

There was only one shower room, a huge black and gold affair that could easily have accommodated us three had we been in station wagons. Anxious to allay my employer's unsavory suspicions, however, I feigned concern with an unspecified flaw in my clothing and waved them ahead.

An awkward few minutes as I waited, holding my towel together while an assortment of squeals, screams, and laughter floated out the shower door. We exchanged rooms, I rejuvenated myself with a twelve-position, vibrating stream of cold water, and returned to find myself thankfully alone in the changing area.

My wallet felt odd as I drew on my pants. I discovered it was sitting in its pocket with the folded end up. This was something I'd never given much thought to before, but I was fairly sure I always put it in the opposite way.

I couldn't be certain, but it struck me that to a man so wealthy he probably never carried a wallet, the position of one in somebody's pocket would be beneath concern.

Nothing else seemed changed. I dismissed the incident as best I could and ascended, level by level, unenthusiastically looking for my host.

"Brown!"

The main floor, and not easy to get to after marinating my legs in steam for so long. He was in the library where we'd had our auspicious first meeting. I helped myself only as far as the arm of a chair, resolving to leave at the earliest opportunity.

"What do you say?" asked Quilp, throwing down a copy of *Scientific American.* "Does God play dice with the universe?"

"I wouldn't think so."

"Why not?"

Hardly the kind of opening conversational gambit that augured well for a quick exit.

"Well…"

Reprieved by a buzz on Quilp's telephone.

"Yes. Ah-hah." He glanced significantly in my direction. "No. No. I'll attend to it."

He hung up. I slipped into the pause and shook his hand. "Guess I'll be going now."

"Oh, and where do you think you're going?"

"Home?"

"I'd wager against it. That call concerned Qina. She's been arrested for shoplifting, in Cleveland."

FORTY-FIVE

I'd been wondering if it were all worth it—Fillmore reducing my end to seventy percent, those large men of Quilp's as competition, lost, crazy Qina, her crazier father, but suddenly it had become easy.

"I think," said Quilp, "we'll teach Qina a lesson. Let's have her spend the night in jail. You can take the first plane in the morning. Satisfactory?"

"Sure."

I wasn't positive I could convince Qina to return with me, but finding her had always been the hardest part of the job.

Ann Adrian booked me out on United Airlines, disarmed an electronic security system behind the front doors, and released me into the outside world.

FORTY-SIX

It was a relief to be rid of Quilp. But though I'd again left him on a high note of anticipation, I had begun to feel in some way diminished. And beyond that, unsettled.

Quilp must figure that if his wife had an appointment with me, she obviously told me things, but he didn't know how much. If he discovered it was Qina that I'd seen, would that make things better or worse?

I hated to deflate the image I'd erected of myself as private detective, but it felt like Quilp murdered Mrs. Quilp and was just keeping me close to find out what I knew.

Had he really gone through my wallet? Probably, since earlier he'd likely set Ann Adrian a similar task.

Did I really want to return the luscious Qina to this demented despot?

I couldn't understand why I was doubting myself. This was not the semilegendary McGee Brown of fearless, East Coast participatory sports journalism.

Quilp seemed able to tap obscure pockets of latent insecurities, insanities, and paranoia and set them in motion—in Qina, in his wife, in Ann Adrian, possibly in that goof Sheriff Mike, possibly in me. Was this the talent that allowed various assholes and villains to rise in our society? I needed Fillmore.

"Enrico's."

"Fillmore."

"Brown, what's shakin'?"

I told him.

"Don't worry about it, man. You're just not used to dealing with crazy people. What we've got here is a family systems issue. In fact, Quilp is clearly the guy that ought to be the patient. He's just putting up a smokescreen, pushing it off on Qina and her mother. Though I admit, from what I've seen of Qina, pretty damn successfully."

"Yeah, well, he's starting to drive me crazy, too."

"Fuck him." Uncharacteristically reckless, Fillmore had obviously been hoisting a few. "C'mon by for a drink."

FORTY-SEVEN

Kloth's Karnival Korner was a topless "klub" a half block up from Enrico's on Broadway. It was owned and run by a New Orleans refugee who insisted on giving his strippers embarrassing appellations in some way peculiar to his hometown—Cajun Carla, Bananas Foster, Hurricane Betsy. I'd recently had a few pleasant encounters with a San Francisco State sociology major known to me only as Leggs Benedict.

Observing Quilp's recreational activities had, I confess, left me feeling a bit randy. I checked my watch, fifteen minutes till show time. If I left right then I could catch her in the act of changing into costume. Factoring our seasonal averages into the equation—two minutes of foreplay, four minutes of volcanic sex—that left plenty of time to stroll over without jaywalking, but not quite enough to discuss her thesis, "The Enduring Cultural Legacy of Michael Jackson."

The doorbell.

I grabbed my jacket, rehearsed a menu of excuses—"Gotta run. Just on my way out. Kind of in a hurry"—and opened the door. I had prepared myself for a number of possible visitors, Rebecca especially, but not for the old man I'd caught spying on me in Quilp's backyard.

"McGee Brown?"

"Yes."

"My name is Jack Himmelfarb. Doctor Himmelfarb. My friends call me Dr. Jack."

"Hello. Uh, I was just…what can I do for you?"

"Do you have a minute?"

"I do have about one minute."

Dr. Jack walked inside and smiled shyly. "Maybe three?"

Visions of Ms. Benedict and myself, breathlessly tangling together on the pile of old Mardi Gras costumes in the Karnival wardrobe room, began to fade unremittingly.

"I'm a dentist," said Dr. Jack quietly.

There was nothing to reply to that, so I didn't. I had to admit, though, the thought that the man I'd caught spying in my rearview mirror was a dentist never crossed my mind. Consequently, we'd now moved up a notch on the bizarreness scale, and I was just that much more interested in why a dentist would be surreptitiously tramping about in Quilp's forest.

"From Providence, Rhode Island."

I knew in which state Providence was located "Yes…?"

"McGee Brown is an unusual name. There used to he a sportswriter in Boston named McGee Brown. A relation by any chance?"

For an instant I feared "dentist" was a cover for bill collector, or maybe summons server. Could my old girlfriend be suing me for breach of promise?

I remembered, however, that my old paper sold well in Rhode Island, and egotism forced me to conclude that I possibly had before me a fan.

"That's me," I answered humbly.

"Ohh, my wife and I used to read your column all the time."

"Thanks, that's always nice to hear." Wait a minute. Why would a dentist come all the way from Rhode Island and follow me around just to let me know he enjoyed my writing? The ghost of John Lennon advised caution.

"We very much enjoyed your series on the Duran-Leonard Superfight." He held up his hands in mock surrender—"*No mas.*"

Ah yes, the "No mas" fight, where the virtually unmarked Duran mysteriously quit in the middle of the eighth round. I'd scored a journalistic coup on that one. Cutting through torrents of speculation, I was the only writer to discover that the spicy New Orleans food had given Duran a sudden attack of diarrhea and, considering the alternative, he'd done the gentlemanly thing and retreated to the locker room. I wondered if Kloth knew that story. I'd tell it to him tonight, if I could just get out the door in the next minute.

"My son was also a journalist," continued Dr. Jack, "a freelancer. He disappeared in Central America."

"I'm sorry." For myself as well as Dr. Jack's son. Flawed though I was, there could be no running out on an old man's sad story.

Dr. Jack passed a silent second of grief. He emerged in a much more deliberate state of mind. "I'd like to ask what your relationship is with Daniel Quilp. I apologize in advance if this line of inquiry seems bold."

Oh, why not. "I'm working as a private investigator. His daughter is missing, I'm trying to find her."

"You gave up your column to move to California and become a private detective?"

"In retrospect, a bad career move, I admit."

Dr. Jack sank into a chair, I bid good-bye to Kloth's enthusiastic backslapping reception to my New Orleans–Roberto Duran story—"Drinks for Brown on the house!"—and to my dancing social historian's "Oh, yes. Yes, baby, yes," and sat down myself.

"Barry, my son, was also always chasing something. For him, the big story, always the Pulitzer Prize in his eyes. Me, I hoped he would get tired of sticking his nose in where it could get broken and just stay home with a job on the *Providence Journal*. Or something in Boston maybe."

I took in Dr. Jack a little more carefully. His clothes were well made, but the deep creases and folds flattening against him begged for twenty extra pounds to smooth into shape.

"But, like you, he was a smart boy," Dr. Jack went on. "He knew what he thought was important, and it was his life."

I, inspired by the reference to lands south of the border, had poured myself a tequila. I offered the same to Dr. Jack, who surprised me by accepting.

"So, he goes to Central America. He's got a big story on the death squads." Dr. Jack gazed sadly into my ceiling. "This is not what I had in mind for my son, to be chasing death squads.

"And he's gone a month, two months, and we get a visit from a man from the State Department. My son is missing. This means dead.

"I couldn't accept that," he continued, slowing his pace. "Not without knowing more. Everybody told me no, but I went to Central America to see, I don't know what. To see what I could see. I found his contact, his source maybe you call him, a man named Sanchez. Very honest, very afraid.

He told me my son was working on a piece about a man known as El Hallero, the finder, the spotter. This was the man that advised the death squads who to 'disappear.' With bribing and threatening and beating, this El Hallero's created his own army of informants.

"Of course, this man had my son killed. I would kill him."

Dr. Jack drank his tequila. I refilled the glass.

"But this was not to be easy. El Hallero traveled a great deal, all over the world. But always alone. He flies his own plane.

"I gave money to a mechanic at the airport, a cousin of Sanchez, to tell me when he arrived. Then I went to where the plane had come from and waited. San Francisco. There's a separate little terminal for private traffic. Sometimes I'd stay in my car, mostly I'd be inside pretending to read flying magazines or killing time at the lunch counter. I couldn't stay twenty-four hours a day, but I knew even if I missed him once, twice, sooner or later I'd see him.

"It took six weeks, a limousine pulled up, the plane landed, and I followed him to the place I saw you." He smiled again. "And you saw me."

This didn't make complete sense. I had no doubt Quilp would sell arms to anyone who asked, but why screw around with internal politics? Protecting some large investment? A coup? CIA stuff? Amusement?

"Now you have it all. I waited for you in Mill Valley, followed you home." Dr. Jack stood wearily. "I know your writing, I feel I know you. I feel I have nothing to fear from you. Perhaps if I need help in some way I can ask you?"

"But what if you're wrong?"

"You know him. Do you think I'm wrong?"

I, in fact, didn't, but, "You can't take the law into your own hands."

"Hmh, I saw those old movies, too. With my son."

"What are you going to do?"

He shrugged. "I don't know. I go there most days, to look."

"That doesn't sound safe, or smart. Sooner or later someone is bound to see you."

Dr. Jack grinned sadly. "I'm a dentist. I don't know how to do it any better."

FORTY-EIGHT

OK. A tough story. One that could potentially throw me into a dilemma. There was only one thing to do. Take Fillmore up on that cocktail.

I ran into Rana Krishna in the hall, and he asked to tag along, "Not to drink. Just to observe the passing parade."

"R.K., in that getup, you're what's going to be observed."

Kermish was working the outdoor night shift. Considering that I'd neglected to pay him on my last visit, he still seemed happy to see me and moved some chairs and tourists around like chess pieces to make room.

I stuck with tequila, Rana Krishna decided on tea. Fillmore came out from behind the bar to deliver them personally.

"Do I have to come to Cleveland?"

"I'll think about it."

"Look, man. I can't always get away that easy. And I have everything figured out anyway." He pulled up a chair. "You're having misgivings about bringing Qina back 'cause you think her old man is dangerous, right? Well, once you get her here, I'll take her on as a patient, a regular patient, and everything will be back on track."

141

"Oh, so now you not only get thirty percent for staying home, you also come away with a wealthy new patient."

"She was my patient to begin with, man."

"No she wasn't, her mother was."

"OK. OK. Twenty-five percent and I don't have to come to Cleveland."

"Twenty."

We shook hands. Fillmore relaxed visibly and sent Kermish back for the tequila bottle.

"You know," he said, "the person I'd really like to get on the couch is Quilp himself."

"You're scared to death of Quilp."

"But I could get a hell of a paper out of him. He looks like a classic bipolar. Always in control, but especially controlling himself. Dominating. Great attention to detail. Heightened sense of organization."

He poured himself a drink. "Quilp would be the measuring stick against which all future manic-depressives were held. Probably only really comfortable in the manic state giving him unlimited energy. Periods of diminished need for sleep. Racing thoughts. Ideas of grandiosity, omnipotency, control, special powers."

"Why?"

"What do you mean why?" Fillmore paused mid-sip.

"Why did Quilp become a manic-depressive?"

"Oh, probably overcompensating an inadequate personality."

"Way too vague."

"How 'bout, spirit broken early in wake of abandonment. Tempted by aphrodisia of power. And the title…will be…"—he downed his drink— "'Polarities and Obsession with Power as Sublimating Receptacles for Manic Energy in an Individual with High Levels of Intelligence.'"

"I'd say you'd struck the perfect balance between science and bullshit there."

Fillmore looked pleased with himself; I'd tell him about the death squads later. Rana Krishna, however, having been left out of the conversation, appeared a little bored. He had taken to staring at a party of large, drunken sailors.

"What are you looking at, you faggot?"

"I'm observing the follies of mankind. And who are you calling faggot, Dumbo?"

This addressed to the speaker, by far the largest and loudest at the table, and a man unfortunately cursed with ears fleeing from the sides of his head. The regulation hat and haircut served only to make matters worse.

"Dumbo!?"

"Ewww," and evil laughs from his shipmates.

"I'll stuff that dress down your throat, ass-wipe."

Dumbo made for us as quickly as the crowd of people, chairs, and tables would allow. Astoundingly, Rana Krishna rose to meet him.

"It's not a dress, it's a sacred robe, Fatso. And it really pisses me off that I've taken a vow of nonviolence to wear it."

This actually stopped Dumbo, probably an ex-altar boy, and he turned to me and Fillmore.

Ever an advocate of religious freedom, I stood myself. "It's true. He's kind of a holy man." Later, when I found out that there was no vow of nonviolence in the MahaVala Kinship Society, that Rana Krishna was, in fact, a sniveling coward, I broke his nose.

"Well, you're no holy man," concluded Dumbo wisely.

I could see that it had been a mistake to rise. "No, but I'm not the one who called you Dumbo either."

My second mistake was selecting a sentence with the word "Dumbo" in it. Other than that, I think I could have made a case for its neutral intent. As the pork roast at the end of his arm sped toward my face, a bolt of psychological insight led me to understand this Dumbo stuff as a bit of unresolved business from his childhood.

He was much drunker than I was, and the blow did little more than glance off the side of my head as I countered to his stomach. He was also, however, a much better bar fighter than I, and his next effort landed me in the lap of a terrified guy wearing expensive, turquoise "sweat" clothes. Hell, as they say, had broken loose.

Two of Dumbo's pals began to chase Rana Krishna under the tables, two more had pounced on Fillmore with genuine violence, a wide, beefy fellow with bosun's stripes had an ugly headlock on Kermish, and the big man himself was charging my way.

Totally intent on avenging the lost honor of the elephants, he missed the look of disbelief in the eyes of everyone at my new table. A small, solitary figure had launched himself from the sidewalk. He half twisted in midair and snapped the heel of his shoe under Dumbo's chin. The elephant boy collapsed where he stood, falling in such a way that not a single innocent bystander was touched.

The men holding Fillmore were too astonished to move, which proved to be a fatal strategy because the small figure was the man whom I instantly accorded the honor of my "favorite patient," Mr. Casbarian. He reached them in two leaps and a shorter jog-step, took the first man out with an elbow, his partner receiving the audible impact of a full-twisting back kick.

I had a good seat with, as I saw it, little incentive to move.

Kermish was released; his tormentor balled his fists and waved them about savagely. Casbarian stepped in, popped a few jabs off his chin, and finished with a whipping right cross.

Two more adversaries remained, but they seemed disinclined to give up their spots under a table of overturned osso buco, petrale in garlic butter, rack of lamb, and penne with Gorgonzola.

Mr. Casbarian dusted himself off—reflex really, he couldn't have accumulated much dust in those brief seconds where he never even lost his balance—and helped me to my feet.

"What ho, Dr. Brown."

"Mr. Casbarian. What are you doing here?"

"Looking for you. One of his" (a gesture to the trembling Rana Krishna) "people told me you'd headed in this direction." The crowd was still buzzing around, and he moved in closer. "I'd like to talk."

But it was not to be. The police had arrived, and we were all hauled down to the North Beach station.

Except two. Enrico was known to all patrolmen in the area, and he successfully pleaded Fillmore's necessity as bartender. Likewise Kermish. He attempted to make a similar case for me, but as I was not an employee, this request was in vain.

It was a slow night, but the booking officers took their time with questioning, processing papers, and drinking Diet Coke. The Shore Patrol eventually came for Dumbo and his gang, and eventually the desk sergeant called the chief, who personally vouched for Mr. Casbarian. But as we were all about to leave I alone was called back.

"Routine questioning."

Mr. Casbarian gave me a card, scribbled down the night-time emergency phone number of the most famous lawyer in San Francisco if I should need assistance, and walked into the night trying on Rana Krishna's mittens.

FORTY-NINE

Lieutenant Scharfman wore a thick wool overcoat, chained-smoked Kools, and shook hands without much interest. He had red hair, a red face, and a red mustache, which he pulled while lost in thought.

"Brown...McGee Brown." He thumbed slowly through some computer printouts on his desk, selecting one. "Unusual name. You are the same McGee Brown that was arrested in Death Valley yesterday morning with...a Dr. Fillmore?"

"I understood that was all cleared up."

"It was, it was...breaking and entering, destruction of personal property, pardoned by the governor, and later vouched for by the owner, Mr. Daniel Quilp." The lieutenant read down the page. "Also a nice testimonial from the arresting officer himself. You must admit," he said, leaning back in his chair, "not a typical case."

I smiled modestly. "Guess not."

"This Daniel Quilp, I'm told, may be the richest man in California. Mrs. Daniel Quilp's body was discovered a few days ago, in a gorilla cage. You know anything about that?"

"No. Well, I heard the gorilla was dead, too."

"That's right, the gorilla was dead, too." He reached for a cup of coffee, ice cold by the expression on his face. I sat quietly as he immediately lit another cigarette to dull the taste.

Two puffs later, "Would you mind telling me how you happened to be in Mr. Quilp's house?"

"I sort of work for him."

"I see. And your job is to destroy his homes."

"No. That was…kind of a mistake."

"Well?"

"Mr. Quilp hired me to find his daughter, who's missing."

"I see. And is that your business?"

"My business?"

"What you do for a living."

"It's kind of…a…"

"Are you a private detective? I thought I knew most of our private detectives."

"This is more like a one-shot sort of deal."

"What is your occupation?"

This guy would never understand life transition facilitator. "I used to be a sportswriter."

"A sportswriter." One more cigarette down, one more up. "Let me get this straight. This fellow Quilp, with all his money, with all his resources, wants to find his missing daughter, so he hires a sportswriter."

Even I had to admit it sounded ridiculous; Lieutenant Scharfman, however, was so proud of his delivery that he unconsciously took another sip of coffee.

"Well?" I didn't know whether he was daring me to laugh or asking me to comment on his comments.

I sort of shrugged my shoulders, but mostly with my hands.

He stood up, planted his fists on the desk, and leaned heavily in my direction. It looked painful.

"Sometimes, I just get suspicious," said the lieutenant. He straightened, examined his knuckles, and put his hands in his pockets in one motion. "When someone dies and there is a great deal of money around, I get suspicious. If that person happens to die in a wild animal cage, I get more suspicious. And every time the victim's husband hires a sportswriter to find the victim's daughter…"

"Even more suspicious."

"That's right."

Lieutenant Scharfman walked to the door, paused with his fingers on the knob. "You're not planning on taking a trip anytime soon, are you, Brown?"

"Tomorrow morning."

"Well, you let me know if…there's anything you think I should know. We've got it down in our books as an accident, but I'm suspicious."

"That would have been my guess."

We shook hands again, the lieutenant fixing me with a steely stare, and I headed directly to Kloth's. Leggs Benedict, dancing particularly well throughout a strobe-light interpretation of Michael Jackson's "I'm Bad," had fallen off the stage in an ill-timed moment of epiphany and twisted an ankle. She was back in her loft with an ice pack and a bottle of Jagermeister.

I went home.

FIFTY

Three o'clock in the morning. I'd gone to the kitchen for something to eat when I noticed a shadow on the wall that was not mine. The apartment was locked, windows shut, blinds down. I stood, unmoving, and watched it glide along the wall and dissolve into the corner.

FIFTY-ONE

United Airlines flight 711 to Cleveland. Stop in Chicago, no change of plane. Chicken Marengo or filet of sole Florentine. Chicken seemed safest, so I took that with an unnecessarily chilled bottle of red wine.

The only guy I remembered well in Cleveland was Maury Bayer, a former backup center for the Browns. We hadn't encountered each other much during his playing years, two, and when he phoned me a while back I'd at first been both surprised and flattered. In some detail Maury praised a last-minute column I'd done, filling in for the regular football reporter, on Cleveland's knack for last-second, come-from-behind wins. He followed through with a pitch for life insurance, three or four times a year. I took a pass on Maury.

Hopkins Airport was on the west side. Qina had been arrested on the east side. The International Humor Convention was in town, and those knuckleheads had rented all the cars. A helpful skycap recommended the Jake & Zack Auto Shack, somewhere in that no-man's-land that surrounds all airports, and I came away with a 1960 MGA, cream with maroon racing stripes, that might have been worth the forty-two dollars a day if it had had third gear and a little bit more of its body. By the time I located the police station in Chagrin Falls, my right leg was coated with a fine spray of oil.

Qina had been caught in the "gourmet" section of Matthew's Buy-Rite pocketing a small pack of Scottish smoked salmon, a jar of red caviar, four bars of Lindt bittersweet chocolate, some olives, an onion, and a tin of pâté. Sixty-eight dollars in all.

Sergeant Gregory was the only man in the office and ready to help. He and the judge, a "Miss Marjorie who's home takin' tea about now," patched things up with a short phone call, letting Qina off for time served.

She came out of her cell seeming fresh—with maybe a tinge of sadness around the eyes.

"Dr. Brown." She checked over my shoulders, decided I was alone, and allowed herself a smile.

We shook hands with the sergeant, climbed into the MG, and Qina directed me through Shaker Heights to a small tavern tucked behind a circular shopping center inexplicably called Shaker Square.

Our booth would have been tight for four but proved comfortable for two. Qina ordered a large Cobb salad, nachos, catch o' the day fish fry, mashed potatoes, diet root beer, chocolate cream pie, and coffee. I'd seen the bartender washing glasses as we arrived; I ordered Rolling Rock and drank out of the bottle.

We made polite conversation. Qina seemed preoccupied with her meal, and as yet, the subject of her ordeal had not come up. A high point for me was when she mentioned that her father owned a piece of the Browns, theorizing that he was in some way responsible for their recent spate of last-second, agonizing defeats; and when she excused herself to the bathroom, I took the opportunity to leave Quilp's address and phone number on Maury's answering machine—anonymously.

Qina took longer than I might have expected, so I amused myself by calling Maury back, leaving first Fillmore's number, then Rebecca Siegelman's, then, in a moment of true inspiration, Lieutenant Scharfman's.

Qina returned looking flushed and fragile. She slid in beside me, squeezed my arm. Red light from an overhead neon beer sign caught a tiny cut on the rise of her cheek, the curve of both breasts as they fell beneath an already mostly unbuttoned blouse.

She ran her finger under my lower lip, touched it briefly to her own. "Dr. Brown," she said, as though supplying the correct answer to a difficult question.

I ran through my options, all of them hinging on either motel rooms or airplanes.

Qina sat back against the side of the booth. She had taken off one shoe and let that leg slide to rest on my lap. "There is nothing sexier than a psychologist."

I motioned for the waitress, asked for our check, but before the first figures in the "ones" column could be combined, Qina halted the computation and ordered a cheeseburger with grilled onions and a strawberry milkshake.

The waitress bounced off toward the kitchen, waving in confirmation of, "Oh, and some french fries please. Well done."

Qina continued to flex and rub her leg along interesting portions of my thighs, but she appeared to be completely absorbed in a *Three Stooges* episode whooping from a TV over the bar.

I waited until commercial. "Come here often?"

"What do you mean?"

"Well it seems like you really love their food."

She giggled. "I'm making a pig of myself."

"No, not really, it's…"

"The police took away all that stuff from the grocery store when they caught me. And I've never gotten much of a meal in jail."

"You mean this has happened before?"

"Yes." Her cheeseburger appeared on the horizon, and she readied the ketchup in anticipation of its landing. "Fourteen times."

"You've been arrested for shoplifting fourteen times."

"I think fourteen." She salted her fries, offered the plate to me.

They were good, crisp and dry on the outside, moist but resistant on the inside.

"But you're incredibly rich. Why would you steal?"

"I'm good at it."

"Caught fourteen times and you call that good?"

"Statistically, I've been doing it every day for the last twenty years."

"But why?"

"What's the difference? I'm bulimic. I'm only going to throw it up again."

FIFTY-TWO

I phoned Fillmore from the airport. He was in Berkeley, but my call was routed from the psychology department to a phone somewhere off campus.

"Stadium."

"Dr. Fillmore, please."

"One sec. Hey, Doc!"

I could hear him puffing up to the phone. "Fillmore here."

"What are you doing in the stadium?"

"Oh, it's you. I shouldn't say. It's confidential." But I could tell that it was going to come anyway. "I have a new client. The bullpen staff of the Oakland A's. Transitory crisis of confidence." He was still in the process of catching his breath, so I got this two or three words at a time. "Think I'm going to get to sit in the dugout and everything, man."

As it happened, I fancied myself something of an expert on pitcher-batter relationships. Though I'd been effectively pigeonholed in the participatory, so-called second-, third-, and even fourth-line sports, my press pass had gotten me into everything, and I was prepared to cover football and baseball if the invitation ever came. Conversely, I doubted that Fillmore even knew the difference between a slider and a slide. In short, this seemed like a logical case for Dr. Brown, Consultant, but as I had irrevocably resolved to bury that personality, the idea had to be buried as well.

"You should see these guys, Brown. They can actually throw balls that curve if they want to."

"No. You better stop them, Fillmore. It sounds like you've hit on the problem already."

"Think so?" he returned proudly. "Hmm. So, what's sha-kin' on your end?"

I told him.

"Bulimia? Don't worry, man. I can cure bulimia with one hand tied behind my back. I've got her already. Disturbance in early childhood. My money's going on unusual eating habits in the family."

"In her family it's hard to imagine normal habits on any front."

"Yeah, with Quilp she probably scored near zero on the fatherly affection scale. So she substituted food for real nurturing. Feeding the hungry heart."

Fillmore was sounding downright buoyant. Just like a boy at the ballpark. "I kind of always hate to cure bulimia, though, man."

"Why?"

"It's the only way I know to have your cake and eat it, too."

FIFTY-THREE

TWA Flight 666 to Denver. Chicken Florentine or filet of sole Marengo. Change of planes to Chuck's Air Service.

"Look, Qina, it was either Chuck or another three-hour delay."

"I don't mind."

Except for a few bad pilot jokes—"Used to have a stewardess, but had to get rid of her 'cause she was too fat. How fat was she? She was so fat that..."—we proceeded to San Francisco without incident. (Though if I'd been forced to hear one more "Two air traffic controllers walk into a bar..." and were able to pilot a plane myself, said incident would have occurred.)

As we made our way through the private aircraft terminal, I saw the restaurant counter where Dr. Jack had spent those many hours waiting for the father of the woman who now walked by my side. I'd left a message for Ann Adrian, and a polished green limo idled immediately outside the glass doors. Resigned to her fate, Qina had said little the whole way across the country, resisting even my witty attempts to enlist her in a campaign to have Chuck's vocal cords removed. But it was not until the chauffeur popped a rear door open for us that I experienced a wave of genuine regret and, possibly, confused conscience. I would have thought myself proficient at dealing with a stray moral qualm, but the internal struggle must have shown in my face.

Qina wiped a few wayward hairs back from my forehead, ran her hand along my cheek. "You're just doing your job. He would have gotten me sooner or later."

She tilted onto her toes, kissed me lightly, and then slid into the amber-lit, black leather chamber. I had my foot on the running board, the chauffeur had his hand protectively on my shoulder. As I bent to swing gracefully to my seat beside Qina, he grabbed a handful of jacket and whipped me back onto the pavement.

"Family matter," the chauffeur said softly. "You don't want to butt in."

Unable to come up with any argument more persuasive than "Hey," I watched them drive away.

"I could have used a lift, you…" Oh, the hell with it. I went back inside the terminal and made two phone calls. One for a taxi, and one to reserve a room at the Big Sur Inn. A short, well-timed vacation, and a fifty-thousand-dollar check when I returned.

FIFTY-FOUR

California sunset. Deepening layers of orange bouncing off the Pacific.

It was dark by the time the cab dropped me at my building, but darker still when I got inside.

Several uniformed police waited in my hallway, watching Lieutenant Scharfman pull his mustache while two men in lab coats passed a clipboard back and forth. An assortment of balding characters in wrinkled sport coats and ill-matched, loosened neckties milled about under an olfactory haze of bad cigars. And there on the ground no more than ten feet from my door was Dr. Jack.

My first take was that he might have been a wino, sleeping off a hard but lucky day of consumption. As I'd never known the elaborate display of locks installed by the MahaVala Kinship Society to operate properly, this had happened before. But up close, it was clear that his head was cocked at an angle that no living body could accept.

From a soft, warm dental office back East, through the bloody intrigues in a foreign land, and the trail ended here.

I told Lieutenant Scharfman what I knew without being asked. Only later did it occur to me that I might in some way have jeopardized my fifty thousand dollars.

"Quilp again, huh." This disturbed the lieutenant. "Doesn't fit with what we got. Simple robbery. Mugger must have heard someone, run off before be could take anything. Old man like this…easy neck to break."

"You're not suspicious?"

"Oh, I'm suspicious, all right." The lieutenant considered the tip of his cigarette as though he hoped to derive some clue from its smoke signals. "Guy like Quilp must make a lot of enemies. But it's backwards. Now, if Quilp were the one who was dead… Why am I telling this to you?"

"Because you instinctively respect my powers of deduction."

"No. I think it's because you're still standing there." He pulled at the cigarette, exhaled in a satisfied smile.

I turned back to Dr. Jack. If there was a Mrs. Jack, the loss of her son and husband in rapid order would as much as kill her also.

"Brown."

"Hmm…? Yes…? What?"

"You, uh, aren't planning on leaving town anytime soon, are you?"

"Tonight."

"Oh. Well…"

"I'll be back in a day or two."

FIFTY-FIVE

I chose the Austin Healey over the Jeep. The temperature was slipping, but I threw on a turtleneck sweater and hit Highway One with my top down.

If Quilp had killed Dr. Jack, Scharfman's job was hopeless. He'd be terminally intimidated from the start, and then Quilp would just deny everything anyway.

What was unsettling to me was where the investigative dentist had met his unfortunate end. Probably he'd simply needed a sympathetic ear and the evening would have wound down to a discussion of my more successful columns. If I had shown up a little earlier, if, say, I'd gotten that limo ride, my presence might possibly have been enough to save the moment. Then again, who knows what the hell went on, and it was not impossible that a timely arrival could have had disastrous consequences for the body and soul of the sometimes Dr. Brown himself.

It was in this vaguely paranoid and certainly morose state of mind that I began to convince myself I was being followed. I had little to go on, a persistent pair of headlights. They were absorbed in the congestion of Monterey and mostly forgotten by the time I pulled into Carmel for coffee.

I flattened down my hair and smoothed the folds in my turtleneck. If Clint Eastwood happened by, I was prepared to be discovered. Since I'd managed to run through journalist, psychologist, and now that I'd returned Qina, private investigator, I was again unemployed.

But two weak cups later, Clint still hadn't showed, so I shifted from would-be movie star back to Pacific Coast idler, and pressed on to Big Sur.

FIFTY-SIX

Due to a slight misunderstanding I wound up with the Honeymoon Suite. At the Big Sur Inn, however, all this really meant was curtains that worked, a slightly larger bed, and a slightly shorter walk down the hall to the bathroom.

I'd arrived just in time to catch the last order of Cornish game hen, and I washed that below with a sleepy bottle of Cabernet. An aspiringly luscious but unnecessarily loud designer from Beverly Hills tried to engage me in conversation from an adjacent table, but when I learned she was attending a life transition facilitation workshop down the road at Esalen, I excused myself and went to bed.

The day had been long; I had no trouble drifting off to sleep. There is little civilization along this particular strip of coastline, and the evenings are black and quiet. If, for some reason, a weary traveler such as myself happens to wake in the middle of the night, it takes a while to place the body coordinates in time and space.

This is what happened to me, and as I lay there debating the relative benefits of a trip to the bathroom or a sip from my bottle of Crystal Geyser mineral water, I became aware of a new presence in the room. I remained still, hoping what

I heard was the ocean and not the respiratory system of another life form.

No really good options presented themselves, but I quickly decided to reject the one where I lay in the dark doing nothing.

I could barely remember the layout of the room, but instinct guided my hand along the night table, up the stem of a lamp, and onto the switch.

"Jesus Christ."

"Hardly."

Quilp sat peacefully in a chair by the door, seemingly oblivious to the impropriety of his intrusion. I, on the other hand, had somehow wound up in a far corner, both hands clutching the sheet to my chin.

Again, no appealing options. I tied the sheet around my waist with whatever dignity was available and sat uncomfortably back in bed. It was several seconds before I could shake the sensation that cold needles had been inserted under my spine.

"You scared the hell out of me."

"Clearly."

"What are you doing here?"

"Completing our bargain."

He took out an onionskin envelope that appeared to have only one thing in it. A check. Mine?

Quilp handed it over. "Pay to the order of Doctor"—I winced, but could foresee no real trouble in that—"McGee Brown. Fifty Thousand and no/100 Dollars."

"I was lucky to find you. Just missed you at your apartment. Couldn't catch you down to Monterey, lost you in Carmel, and after a few wrong guesses, spotted your car in the parking lot here."

"Huh. Well, great. I wish you could have…"

"Waited till morning? Sorry. Too busy for that."

"Ahh."

"What are you doing in Big Sur?"

"Just…relaxing."

"I hate just relaxing. I hate Big Sur."

"Ahh."

Quilp had one of those large, flat portfolios favored by photographers and graphic artists on his lap. He worked the zipper slowly around its perimeter as he spoke. "My daughter said I was evil."

"About that. Dr Fillmore has…"

"Then the police came by. Briefly. A Lieutenant Scharfman. Attempting to question me concerning a murder. An old man. At your apartment."

"Oh, that was…"

"No. I understand." Quilp slid a large sketchpad onto one knee, flipped through the pages, and set to work with a sharpened piece of charcoal.

"I thought I was most generous with you," he continued. "Perhaps I even dared hope that our lively exchanges of information had something about them approaching friendship. But it's clear to me now that you take this old man's rantings as something more valuable. That when my sadly disturbed daughter accuses me of the most heinous crimes, it's she that wins your sympathies."

Since Quilp still had ample time to stop payment on my check, I'd been concentrating on projecting charm and sincerity. Sympathy had not occurred to me. As I tried my best to push my features into friendly, sad-eyed compassion, Quilp closed one eye and sort of pointed his finger at various parts of my face.

"I'm sorry, but what are you doing?"

"A habit. Hobby."

"You're drawing a picture of me? In a sheet?"

"Does it bother you?"

The check. "Well, it's…ah, no. Not…really. I guess."

"Do you believe," asked Quilp, bearing into a series of long, bold hues unseen to me, "that I killed this man?"

"Oh, that guy," I said, sidestepping. "A pretty nice guy actually. Only met him once though. Seemed nice. He had some idea that his son…"

"His son."

"Right. His son and you…"

"His son," said Quilp, "was taken by a jaguar in the moonlight near a waterfall the Indians call *mbele.*"

"Pardon me?"

"Killed, by a jaguar."

"How would you know that?"

"The waterfall becomes a stream, the stream empties into a pool where soldiers linger too long over cook fires and talk too much. They heard his screams." A moment here while he appraised his work at arm's length.

"Odd," Quilp continued, "that the police never questioned you more closely." He looked up from his page. "About the father."

"What do you mean?" Dr. Brown, sensing dangerous curves ahead.

"The body was found on your doorstep as I understand it."

"Well, so?"

"Wouldn't you kill someone who was a threat to your existence?"

"That's ridiculous. I didn't even know him until the other day."

"I was led to believe you knew each other back East."

"No, no he was…"

"How else would he find you?"

"Followed me from your place."

Quilp produced a thick folding knife, black with worn grooves that acted as finger grips. He tested its sharpness against a thumb and, satisfied, stroked it repeatedly the length of his charcoal. "A hypothetical here, Brown. Let's say I was the devil." He smiled thinly. "Oh, not a high-ranking devil, of course, but certainly one resourceful enough to kill, say, the stray old man here, or a woman with a bad heart there. A gorilla, possibly. Would that worry you?"

Crazy or dangerous? Both probably. We were alone, he had a knife, and I was naked. Great.

If he were truly insane, all bets were off. But if it was only that he thought I had something on him and was trying to scare me off…I figured I ought to bluff.

"No, not that much."

"See, now that worries me. What's to be done with you?"

"Well, you said 'if.'"

"No. I said 'let's say.' Frankly, you worry me altogether. You didn't seem quite 'right' somehow at our last meeting."

Quilp flourished a final bit of shading and threw down his charcoal. He held his knife by the point, drummed the butt on his knee. The drawing fell to one side. I didn't think he captured my eyes, but the hair was good.

For the past few minutes, on some secondary but insistent level of thought I'd been wondering about my pants. There had been various plans, all banking on the possibility that I might surreptitiously grab them with my toes and pull them into position under the sheet. Now, as vanity forced me to examine the fruits of Quilp's labor tossed aside on the floor, I recognized a flap of material hanging to one side of his chair. And worse, as the fuzzy memories of undressing rose from the hinterlands, I realized that Quilp was sitting not only on my pants, but also my fresh shirt, my jacket, and my favorite pair of sunglasses.

"Perhaps," said Quilp suddenly, "you were actually hit by that piano and all this is merely an elaborate, extended, flashing fantasy as you fall under the blow and the force cracks your skull toward death."

The effect of this was, of course, powerful, and intensified by its abrupt delivery into a long silence marked only by the slow, periodic crashing of the Pacific. Three things happened—my mouth froze in an idiotic, ingratiating smile, my testicles shriveled, and my brain both froze and shriveled. "Nice portrait. Have you ever shown any of your stuff? Professionally. In a gallery or anything?"

"And I some seed of my wife's tale, seized, conjured whole, playing a role that exists in your mind's eye alone. A projection of some…"

"How's Qina?"

That one slowed him. He stared at me a moment, then the window, then a corner of the ceiling, then me again. Folding his sketchpad, he grabbed the portfolio by its handles and stood. "Resting."

"Ah, good."

He opened the door, backed a step into the hall. "Locked in her room."

"Ahhh."

"Dead, actually."

FIFTY-SEVEN

In the event that Quilp might decide to stop payment on my check, I'd set an early alarm, calculated to land me beneath the porticos of the nearest Bank of America well before the doors opened. But I never got to hear it.

As I lay awake, watching my Casio's digital colon pulse between the hour and minutes before sunrise, a knock at the door.

Lieutenant Scharfman, a policeman, two huge men in white uniforms, me in a sheet.

"Good morning, Brown."

With certainty, I knew it wasn't.

"We have here a 5150 form, signed by myself, a Dr. Einstein, and Mr. Quilp who, as honorary fire chief of Burbank is officially designated by the State of California as a mandated worker, as I am myself, to sign papers authorizing involuntary committal."

I said, "What?" but not loudly.

"May I see that?" He pointed.

The check, my alarm clock acting as paperweight. I ignored the request. Lieutenant Scharfman helped himself.

"What's going on?"

The lieutenant smiled gravely to himself, folded the check into a large manila envelope. "In view of the testimony and evidence, Dr. Einstein has concluded that you are a danger to yourself and others. Mr. Quilp and I make up the necessary three signatures."

"What are you talking about?"

One of the men in white had produced a dripping syringe from the folds of his jacket. That, Qina's death, the interment of my check, and the prospect of doing battle in a sheet, all bespoke the inevitability of a long, hard slide.

"You extorted this money from Mr. Quilp, attempting to blackmail him over his daughter's arrest. You think you're a psychologist. You think Quilp is the devil. You attempted to rape his secretary. You stole his Jeep Cherokee. You took off all your clothes and forced your way into his steam bath. You start fights in bars. You break into houses. You break out of jails. You accuse Quilp of killing his wife and this man he doesn't even know, Dr. Himmelfarb, and in all probability you perpetrated those murders yourself." He lit a cigarette, exhaled for emphasis. "And that's only in the last few days."

"Wait a second. This is insane!"

"That's the issue."

"No, you don't understand. Quilp is the lunatic here, and Einstein is Quilp's mistress."

"Uh-huh. Look, Brown, I don't know much about this psychology stuff, but they told me that denial was part of your mental condition."

"What would I do if I were innocent?"

"So you're telling me none of this stuff is true?"

"Well, it's...there's...things just aren't the way they sound. Quilp's got all the facts twisted." I noted the look of perceptive forbearance on the faces of the men in white coats. "Lieutenant, you know me now. Do I seem like a dangerous, crazy person to you?"

He pulled at his mustache. "I've met you twice. Once in a police station, and once at the scene of a crime."

I groaned audibly. The syringe moved a step closer. "Look, let me put on my pants." I didn't know why, but I was sure this would make me feel better. It didn't. As I lifted them off the chair, Quilp's knife flipped out and stuck heavily in the floor. The lieutenant and I smiled at each other.

"That's Quilp's knife," I said, watching it quiver.

"Of course."

"No, it really is."

Lieutenant Scharfman handed me my squashed shirt. "Brown, I can't say I dislike you. And I admit you don't seem much like a murderer to me. But like I told you, I don't know this psychology shit. My feeling is that you need help, and my advice it to take it."

"I don't need any help. I just need some time to explain all this."

"You'll have plenty of time."

"Hey! Hold everything. Call Fillmore."

"Fillmore? Fillmore. Wasn't he the guy you broke out of jail with in Death Valley?"

"Fillmore. He's a professor of psychology at Stanford. And Berkeley. You met him."

"When?"

"That other night at Enrico's. The fat guy. He was the bartender."

"The bartender is a psychologist."

"That's right."

"What about that character in the robes? Also a psychologist?"

"No, he's with the MahaVala Kinship Society."

"Oh," said Lieutenant Scharfman, turning to the others, "with the MahaVala Kinship Society."

The attendants' eyes rolled in response. A smirk from the cop.

"You sure hang out with an interesting crowd, Brown."

My pants were on, I held the shirt loosely in my hands gauging speed and distance—the window, the door, the parking lot, the relative position of policemen, white uniforms, the luscious designer whispering thrillingly to her roommate in the hallway beyond. The halfback in me thought I had a chance. My mistake was checking my pocket for car keys.

The white suits caught the move and its implications immediately. Experience hurled them across the room. Including the policeman, a good six hundred pounds of restraint. A sharp pain inside my left elbow, and a warm wash spread through my chest and pulled me under.

FIFTY-EIGHT

In the lands to the east, beyond the Nimitz Freeway, beyond a tall, ragged stretch of the Diablo Range lie the ancient, sprawling, weather-scarred confines of Barronville State Home for the Hopelessly Insane.

It is always shocking to come upon one of these anachronisms in California. In this case, a decaying, pale yellow complex of squat institutional buildings redolent of the Deep South at the turn of the century. And this no more than a quarter tank of gas in even the most unforgiving Cadillac from the skyline of San Francisco.

I, of course, saw none of it as, at the time of my approach, I was flat on my back in the rear of a California state issue van.

I awoke in a room only twice the size of my bed, which was small. A number of restraints seemed to have been recently removed, the purplish-tending bruises around my wrists and ankles remaining as signatures.

The ceiling was high, and I had one window, in the door, with bars. There were rusting drains in each corner and a few blankets stacked on the floor, beige with beiger stripes.

My head felt large, but its interior seemed clear enough, so I swung off the bed, stood, and walked to the window, two steps.

Outside my door, across a narrow hall, was another door. Almost identical to mine, this one had a hinged wooden flap bolted over the window.

Not a particularly captivating vista, but as I was about to turn back to bed I saw the door shudder. Then again. And throughout the twenty minutes or so I watched, as though the poor soul inside—I assumed the poor soul, but for all I knew it could have been Jimmy Hoffa in there—was repeatedly rushing the length of his room, four steps, in an attempt to smash a shoulder through. Would this eventually be me?

I returned to bed and reviewed my situation. I felt nearly bad enough about Qina to toy with the guilty notion that there was some bizarre, deserving form of justice at work. Nearly. What concerned me mainly was that I was undoubtedly in an insane asylum, and for whatever reasons, if certain forces had conspired to get me in here, did I belong?

I thought not, of course, but there was always the possibility that the wheels of state had spun correctly. Beyond doubt, Quilp had orchestrated this mess, but Lieutenant Scharfman had made a good case. The last few days had been fairly insane.

But then, as I got up to watch the door across the hall some more, I had a moment of frightful clarity. At the same instant I realized with joy that this place must be full of crazy people, truly blubbering, ranting, hallucinating, screaming, delusional, crazy people, and that I was not, could not be among their number, that I must be strong, I also realized that crazy people really scare me.

I was among the wild ones now, and though I knew myself to be sometimes rash and, admittedly, eccentric, at that moment I felt only a truly sane person could be so thoroughly frightened.

Daunted by the prospect of this enforced companionship, although relieved also by confirmation of my own sanity, for the present anyway, I crept onto my bed again—the only thing I had to do really, besides counting the blankets or looking out the window one more time—and watched the paint pebbles on my wall. Then, some noise outside, and before I could get up, a scrape as a tray was slid into my room. I stepped over it in time to catch a slice of shadow disappearing down the hall.

OK, a translucent, processed turkey sandwich on white bread with what could have been either a little watery mayo or chemical secretions from the meat itself, a paper cup of grapefruit juice, unsweetened, and a note.

Doctor Brown. Welcome to Barronville. Would you like to see me? Since you can have neither pencil nor pen nor any sharp instrument, so don't ask, please indicate by tearing the appropriate

YES   NO

and sliding this back under the door.

Doctor Limbus-Edgington

FIFTY-NINE

Doctor Limbus-Edgington was a thick-boned, buxom woman in her early fifties. I'd been brought to her office by three beefy guys whom she dismissed with a couple of grand, backhanded waves.

The door clicked us alone. Dr. Edgington inclined her head, indicating a lone chair in the middle of the room, and as I advanced to take it, she matched me step for step. Turning toward her, more in surprise than anything else, I stopped short. She did not, walking directly into me and, once physical contact had been established, took me in her arms and kissed me wetly on the lips.

"One rule. I get to kiss anybody I want...sit. Sit, Dr. Brown. That's what the chair is for."

I did. The doctor slid behind her desk with a strange, backward step that looked much like the Michael Jackson moonwalk. "Ha ha. You see, I can't turn my back on you. You must prove to me that you are worthy of my trust. But," she sat with satisfaction, "you know you can trust me because I kissed you."

It had been my intention to pin certain hopes on this Doctor Limbus-Edgington and, needless to say, thus far these hopes had found no purchase.

"So. Do you trust me?"

"I…"

Dr. Edgington made a quick note on her steno pad, licked her lips, and stood again.

"I do. I feel I can trust you. Somehow, I feel I can. Yes."

"Good. Good." She smiled modestly. "A new theory." She remained standing and, in spite of her earlier dictum, turned to survey her diplomas on the wall behind. Doctor of Psychiatric Edification, University of Nancago. Member, Royal Poldavian Academy. Honorary Kentucky Colonel.

An intercom buzzed. "Yes? Yes," and a louder. "Yes!"

The door opened, and an orderly rushed in holding a starched green bundle roughly the size of the Kentucky honorarium. He laid it in my lap. A uniform.

"That will be all, Scott." He backed off in what I now assumed was the gait of choice here in Barronville.

I was still in the wrinkled clothes Quilp had used as a cushion back in Big Sur. But not for much longer.

"If you please, Dr. Brown," said Limbus-Edgington, pointing a red fingernail.

"No, I'd rather…"

"Show trust."

"But this is all mistake. I don't belong here. Seriously. Just let me…"

"This conversation can end now!" And softer, touching the more delicate keys. "We must erect a bridge of trust."

I tried to do this as I imagined a flagrantly normal person might. Neither too modest nor too bold, I stepped behind the chair, turned 135 degrees sideways, and executed the change, continually alert for any noise that might mean Edgington was on the move again.

The shirt was merely large; my pants, however, were so hopelessly oversized that there was sufficient material to knot up at the waist and achieve a serviceable snugness. A pair of thin, white plastic sandals had been wrapped in one of the legs, and when I slid into these, the transformation was complete. I was an inmate. And if anyone were to judge solely by the cut of my jib, an essentially ridiculous one.

In an attempt to display this laughably poor fit to the doctor, thereby demonstrating my clear, sane perspective on the whole affair, I stepped to one side of the chair, grabbed the material at each thigh, and spread it out to its full girth. Since this was a novel, unfamiliar move to me, too late I realized that, hunched over with my pant wings fully extended, from the doctor's point of view, I was…curtsying.

I was in an insane asylum, wearing a crazy person's clothes, trying to impress a madwoman by acting like a madman. I climbed back into my chair and smiled; she did the same.

"Now, Dr. Brown, how can I help you?"

Too shaken by my present circumstances to be creative, I chanced, "I'm in trouble."

"I see—you feel troubled."

"No, I'm really in trouble. I think my employer's trying to frame me."

"Pardon me?"

"I said I think my employer's trying to frame me."

"You think your employer's trying to frame you."

"That's right. I need help."

"You believe you need help."

"Oh no."

"Yes?"

"Unconditional positive regard. Rogerian therapy. Please stop repeating everything I say."

"Ah yes." Dr. Edgington thumbed through what must have been my file. "Your obsession. You believe you are a psychologist."

"No. No, I don't. That was just…I don't really think I'm a psychologist."

"You don't really think you're a psychologist."

"No."

"But you had a patient. This employer's wife…who later turned up dead."

"I never met her. I knew the daughter, who I met when she pretended to be her mother, his wife."

"Yes…and do you think this employer, this Daniel Quilp, is the devil?"

Hah. "No."

"No? Then how did I get this information?"

"His daughter thinks he's the devil."

"Not his wife."

"Her too."

"I see. And you exploited the situation to extort the fifty thousand dollars."

"No, I earned that."

"From Mr. Quilp, your employer."

"That's correct."

"By murdering this dentist you believed to be his enemy."

"No, I didn't do that. He did."

"Quilp did it." Dr. Edgington switched to red pencil, printed *Quilp*, and connected it to various parts of the page with a serious of arrows.

"That's right. He told me so. Sort of."

"Why?"

"Quilp had the dentist's son killed in Central America because he found out he was in charge of the death squads."

"Who was?"

"Quilp."

"Quilp told you this?"

"No, the dentist did."

"But Quilp told you he murdered the son."

"No…he tried to make me think a jaguar did it."

"And the wife?"

"A gorilla."

"You didn't kill anybody."

"That's right."

"What did you do?"

"I didn't do anything."

"You're an innocent man."

"Of course."

She pulled out a couple of Xeroxes. "Burglary and vandalism in Furnace Flats, assault and battery and disturbing the peace at a bar called Enrico's in San Francisco…ah, I see you think you're a private eye." The doctor actually looked impressed. "Do you carry a gun?"

"No, I don't carry a gun."

"Just a knife."

"A knife? No. That wasn't my knife. It was Quilp's."

Limbus-Edgington sighed. "Dr. Brown."

"Just Brown."

She squinted, circled something on my arrest record. "All right. Brown. Allow me to provide you with insight. It is a mark of the paranoid schizophrenic that he takes all facts, all objective realities, and somehow bends them to fit what he believes to be the drama of his life...to illustrate, the patient who was in here before you used to roam the alleys of Los Angeles, picking up scraps of paper and garbage believing they were clues left for him by an international secret society. He felt he was being tested, and that once he was able to make sense of these clues, he would be asked to join this society. By the time he was brought to Barronville, he had eight trunks full of the most filthy, meaningless junk, and seventy-four notebooks interpreting their meaning."

"You put me in the same category as him?"

She shrugged her shoulders.

"Look, Dr. Edgington. Please just call Dr. Fillmore. You can get him at either the Berkeley or Stanford psych department. He'll clear everything up. Really. I honestly haven't done anything wrong, or anything even crazy. I know on the surface it all seems a bit hard to believe, but Dr. Fillmore will back my version of this."

"Dr. Fillmore is your psychologist."

"No. No."

"Also a private detective?"

"No. Dr. Fillmore is really a doctor. Please, let's just call him now."

"Fillmore," she said as she ran her finger down one of the forms in my folder. "Fillmore. Fillmore..."—a triumphant look—"ah, the bartender."

"No. He is a bartender, yes. But he's mainly a psychologist. But not mine."

"Dr. Brown…I'm sorry, 'doctor' seems somehow to fit. Mr. Brown, I must acquaint you with certain facts."

"Yes? What?"

"Involuntary committal requires a mandatory seventy-two-hour hold, after which time there is a hearing with all concerned parties. However, the initial committal can also be extended for fourteen days with the proper certification which, in your case, has already happened."

"Seventeen days?"

"You'll be returned to your room for tonight. If you can refrain from masturbating, swearing out loud, and playing with your food, you'll be taken into population tomorrow, to the locked ward which we affectionately call the flight deck."

"Jesus Christ!"

Dr. Edgington wrote that down.

SIXTY

In the dream Quilp took me to a club, a gaming establishment, palatial, pretentious, swank. We played recklessly (my fifty thousand dollars), laughed, drank, a beautiful woman massaged my gambling arm.

As we left, the man who ran the establishment called me aside and asked us not to come again. Quilp made an appeal; I attempted one also but was so shocked I could do little. Nonetheless, the man returned inside, came back with some of the patrons and a few waiters, and told me there was no mistake, sorry.

I walked the streets, Quilp at my side. Somehow this struck the core of me. No matter how I looked or dressed (I was in my underwear), no matter the circumstances, somehow the essential, winning, charming Brown should be in evidence. It began to rain.

Quilp suggested a cafe. I was reluctant to enter. He pulled me inside; we were served two of those green cocktails. A newsboy tossed a paper on the table—"Rebecca Siegelman wins Pulitzer Prize"—and I began to get suspicious.

It was too pat. In some safe, interior place I knew this could not be. Quilp seemed to sense that I sensed this.

I got up to leave but found myself delivering a speech having to do with man's inhumanity to man, so ordinary, so profoundly dull that I cleared out the cafe.

A nightmare, but it felt all wrong. Even as I slept, I knew that either present circumstances had propelled me into a whole new, considerably more unsettling strain of nightmare, or that someone, something else was influencing my dreams.

SIXTY-ONE

The flight deck. A long, narrow room painted the color of my uniform. I was assigned a bed—one of twenty-six, two rows of thirteen each—all the way in the rear, against the far wall. Good because in case of trouble I could easily protect my back, bad because in case of trouble I'd be trapped, twenty-five beds from the door

But would there be trouble? The only sounds were whimpers from a circle of patients locked in a whining debate having something to do with whether George had been the real force behind the Beatles.

I was led past, and virtually no notice was taken of my passing. Here a patient sleeping, there one dozing, one smoking, one on the floor twisted up like a pretzel, two waltzing, three playing checkers, one reading *Time* magazine upside down, one doing something that might have been yoga, and most of the rest watching those just mentioned.

It was immediately obvious why my assigned bunk was the least popular, most available in the room. On the one across sat a man with a purple crayon and a notebook, and all about him, stacked against the wall, pushed under his bed, under my bed, piled around and between the beds, were a number of trunks. Each was identified in dark red script, Rudolph 1, Rudolph 2, and on to Rudolph 9, which I had to step over to reach my tiny sanctuary.

I made as little noise as possible, and he remained absorbed in his pages.

"Dang."

Next to Rudolph, grinning broadly, was the only patient in the room wearing a hat. A forest ranger hat.

"Dr. Brown?"

Now suddenly the center of attention, I managed a simpering smile.

"Dr. Brown!"

"Hi," and then to the room in general, "hi."

A substantial shock, running into someone I knew, but the State had made no mistake here.

Sheriff Mike.

"Brown?" Rudolph switched colors.

"That's him. Shit, yeah," said the sheriff. "How are ya?" His right arm was taped to his side, and as he came over to visit he held that shoulder gingerly.

"Sheriff Mike?"

"Shit, yeah." And to an approaching attendant, "Hey, pardner."

The attendant grunted in return, pulled out a blue marking pen, and wrote 3AM on my forearm. Another shouted, "Attention," and Sheriff Mike guided me into place at the foot of my bed. The patients dawdled their token resistance but seemed to have long ago caved into the inevitability of their routine. The last to fall in line was a short fellow wearing a pillowcase as a shirt.

"Roll call!"

A few seconds of silence, and then the guy with the pillowcase stepped forward and yelled, "I'm Spartacus."

Next, the *Time* magazine reader: "I'm Spartacus." The smoker, the waltzers, and down the rows to Rudolph, who winked at me knowingly and pointed finger circles at the side of his head while intoning, "I'm Spartacus."

Clearly, a truce had been reached satisfactory to all parties as the attendant in charge merely kept count of each Spartacus.

All eyes on me, expectantly, as I contributed my "I'm Spartacus." The cheers followed, and I perceived myself one more step removed from the outside world.

Next on the program was a march to the dining hall where we were all treated to lukewarm, lumpy mush, damp slices of white bread, and pale pink Kool-Aid.

Back to the flight deck, which I was depressed to discover had already, on this, my return visit, begun to acquire that familiar feeling that comes with home.

At breakfast, Sheriff Mike had informed me that my bunk in the "lower thirteen" put us on the same softball team, but he'd have to sit out today's game as he'd recently injured his shoulder trying to break down a door. Rudolph listened carefully, made a few notes.

By my calculations, Mike could have been here no more than a couple of days—no doubt our session together had inspired him to who knows what heights of imbecility—yet had already installed himself as a figure of some popularity.

Since his injury relegated Mike to the sidelines, the team had accorded him indefinite tenure as manager. Unfortunately, however, as we trotted off to take the field later that day, Mike appeared to have some trouble with his transmitter, and was forced to spend the first few innings trying to clear things up with army headquarters.

Spartacus was, of course, team captain, and in that capacity turned over the managerial duties to Rudolph, who used the opportunity to deliver an astoundingly complex and far-reaching pep talk. One, I might add, that seemed to be not only understood but enthusiastically received by all save myself.

I was given second base, an assignment that secretly delighted me since, as a left-hander, I'd spent many a summer afternoon in the outfield, well removed from the real action.

The lower thirteen prevailed. I myself going three-for-five, including an inside-the-park home run when two of our opponents' infielders engaged in a game of keep-away with their own teammates.

During the post-game celebration, however, a couple of troubling moments. The first when Rudolph showed me a wall one could scale to reach the women's side where he claimed to be conducting an ongoing, rapturous affair with a petite blond envoy from the planet Vassar-79. Beyond the wall, parked in the shade of a small cottage set apart from the main buildings, was a limousine that looked disturbingly familiar.

But worse, while the team was stacking away our equipment, Spartacus pulled me out of umpire attendant earshot and informed me that the blue 3AM on my forearm, which I'd shoved well down the list of my considerations, meant I was scheduled for a session of electroshock at three in the morning.

SIXTY-TWO

"Dr. Edgington," I said, wiping the lipstick from my cheek. "Please."

"Ahh, Mr. Brown." She watched me carefully to see if I objected to the loss of title. "Trust me. I know what I'm doing."

"I trust you," I lied, "but you can't give me electroshock before my hearing. Can you?"

"This is going to help you at your hearing. You will make a much better showing, I am sure."

"But I don't want it. It's dangerous." I shot to my feet for oratorical effect. Edgington flinched, so I thought better of it and lowered myself back down, into a posture of utter calm, easy control. "I'm telling you again," I said evenly, "this is all a mistake. I am not crazy, I've done nothing wrong, and I don't belong here."

"Ah, ha ha. Everyone is a little crazy, no? And," she said, picking up a chart, "perhaps you belong here more than you've considered. According to these reports you've cooperated right from roll call, made several friends already, hit a home run in baseball, and in general seem to be fitting into our routine nicely."

"No, no. The reason for that is…" What was the reason for that?

"I've already given considerable thought to your case, and the pathological sources of your feeling about Mr. Quilp. In fact, we discussed it no more than an hour ago."

"We?"

"Your Mr. Quilp is quite concerned. I see that surprises you. But please, he has assured me that he will withdraw his personal portion of the complaints against you, and even assist in your defense if you cooperate here.'"

"Whose idea was electroshock?"

"Why, his possibly. Or mine. Or Dr. Einstein. No matter. It's quite usual in problems like yours."

"Like mine? And what exactly do you see as my problem?"

The doctor smiled. "You will be happy to know that even at this early stage, I've made a diagnosis I'm quite satisfied with. And I believe I will tell. You shall know your illness as the first step to understanding it."

She placed the fingertips of both hands together at a point just below eye level and abandoned me in a dialectical cul-de-sac: "You have an innocence fixation."

SIXTY-THREE

I was placed in a holding cell across the hall from Dr. Edgington's office. One chair, bolted to the floor, and a large window with thick wire mesh.

It seemed my best chance lay with the attendants. Assuming Dr. Edgington to be above a mundane, mechanical procedure like electroshock, I further assumed, hoped, she would he asleep by three a.m., home, certainly. I had, in the course of my travels, occasion to acquire the knack of bribing minor Third World bureaucrats; in my work, of bribing coaches, athletes' girlfriends, other sportswriters; and in my role as male, maître d's and doormen.

I was confident that any state employee would cheerfully falsify institutional records for the promise of a few hundred, and if need be, a few thousand dollars. The difficulty would lie in overcoming their presumption that I was insane, and as such, could not be trusted to come through with the funds in question. What was required here was a fast, forceful start.

Rehearsing my opening lines—"Gentlemen, I have a proposition…"—I stepped to the window, laced my fingers through the mesh, as I was sure many a sad soul had done before me; and suddenly, in the gathering darkness, there she was. Walking the grounds, barefoot, in a diaphanous white robe, smiling up, it seemed, wistfully at my window. Qina. No wonder her death had never been somehow added to the list of my misdoings. It was just a ploy of Quilp's to throw me off balance before the arrival of Lieutenant Scharfman.

She moved slowly, considering each step, feeling the grass between her toes, a breeze catching the folds of her wrap.

I was seized from behind, thrown backwards, and strapped to a narrow gurney.

"Wait! Wait a second..." was the only part of my plan I managed to squeak out before a coarse strip of adhesive tape was placed over my mouth.

SIXTY-FOUR

Wheeled along a corridor, then another, down a ramp to the basement, a series of left turns, a pair of swinging doors, another left, two rights. All this flat on my back, watching the overhead fixtures flick by.

"Mmpf."

The electroshock chamber. A tangle of cables, switches, dials with ominous red and orange zones, most of it appearing to predate the Geneva Accords.

With the wordless departure of the attendants, it was clear I needed a new plan. Squirming free of my restraints was not possible. Likewise levitating, shrinking, and becoming invisible, although, in desperation, I tried them all. In short, there seemed no strategy available capable of handling even the simplest of the difficulties with which I was now handicapped.

So I lay there for a long time, long enough to track the Belt of Orion wheeling past a barred window high on the wall, waiting for somebody to shave my head or lather me up or whatever, when I heard voices in the hall.

The door opened behind me; they walked in and arranged themselves around my bed. Dr. Limbus-Edgington, Dr. Einstein, Ann Adrian, Daniel Quilp.

"You see." Dr. Edgington. "Quite safe. Quite prepared."

"Quite," said Quilp. "Always best to go for speed in these cases. Don't you agree, Dr. Einstein?"

"Umm." Einstein nodded her assent.

"Brown," said Ms. Adrian. She took in the novel fit of my pants, the curves of sweat spreading under my arms, a thick grass-and-dirt stain down my right side—the result of a nicely executed, late-inning slide into third base.

"Sad." She turned to the others. "He seemed fine a few days ago."

"Mmpf."

"Yes." Quilp was squeezing one hand with the other. "Dr. Edgington, a favor?"

"Certainly, Mr. Quilp."

"A few moments alone with my friend." He opened the door, smiled them out with a scoop of the arm and an unctuous, "Ladies…"

"Yes. Certainly. Come, Ms. Adrian, Dr. Einstein. I'll make some tea."

Quilp pushed on the door several seconds longer than necessary, waiting till the tap of footsteps faded behind distant corners. He spun around to face me, already laughing. "Ha ha. Not only is she not a doctor," he spread his hands, struggling against his mirth to force out the words, "her name isn't even Einstein. I did it to be funny." His joke doubled him up, repeatedly, and as he tried to control himself, laughing and sort of goose-stepping around the room, he looked like one of those shooting gallery bears that rear up with every hit. He tapered down to, "Oh, my. My, my. Heh heh, yes," and began to finger the various controls.

"Umpfpf."

"Oh, stop worrying. I don't even know how to operate this thing."

"Umm. Ummm!"

"All right. What?" He peeled back the tape, but just an inch or two. I was forced to talk out of the side of my mouth, like Popeye.

"Look. Quilp. I know you're not about to help me out of here, but could you just get Edgington to call off this electroshock?"

"Ha. Dr. Limbus-Edgington." He smoothed me shut again. "What an asinine, bovine, addle-brained old bag that one is. In fact, I've got her convinced that with my financial support, Barronville may one day become the axis around which all psychologists, and psychologies, are forced to spin." He folded his arms. "You see, Brown, people are basically good. Circumstances make them bad. I create the circumstances."

"Ummm!"

"What?" He picked up a corner of the tape, but kept hold this time so I decided to keep my part brief.

"Please?"

"Ha. You expect sympathy from the devil? Can't, I'm afraid. You see, I don't often get my hands dirty. I usually just set things in motion from a distance—those subscription cards that fall out of magazines, rebates, call-waiting, daytime talk shows, leaf blowers, wind chimes, twenty-one ions of C-4 plastique explosive to Qaddafi, frequent flyer programs, the prevent defense...but happening upon that annoying old man in front of your door was too good an opportunity to waste."

"What...?"

"I know. You think I'm trying to drive you crazy."

"No, no."

"I really am the devil."

"I understand...like belonging to one of those satanic religions."

"No! Vanity forced me to check them out, naturally, but they don't have a clue. I find them unimaginative, frankly."

He hung his face over mine, searching for a reaction. I groped for one other than the ones I was feeling—panic, despair, and in my irrepressible role as psychologist, a con- noisseur's appreciation of a virtuoso performance.

"You see..." Quilp began to swagger around the room using his hands to help him search for the right words, "...these myopic, ignorant, vapid historians and insipid, thick-headed economists believe events are cyclical. Non- sense. They are merely tied into my itinerary. Do you know, the Nazi party came about purely as a result of my having extended business in Germany at that time."

Smoothly now. Oh, by the way... "Would you mind unty- ing me?"

"I have it at present so that the man on the street can't talk to a strange woman because she'll think he might be a rapist. He can't talk to a strange man because he'll think he might be a scam artist or a mugger. He can't talk to strange children because they'll think he might he a kidnapper." Quilp raised the volume a notch. "I am the spirit that denies. I am the enemy of thought, I am the ill wind that..."

"Just the arms. I can do the rest myself."

"Shut up."

I did.

"I don't have any superpowers, you understand. Otherwise I could just destroy anything I wanted and that would be it. I'm forced to rely on style." Quilp cheeked his watch, picked up his pace. "But as you know, things could get a little too uncomfortable for me around here. I'm pulling up stakes in Mill Valley tonight. Heading, as they say, for parts unknown."

"What happens to me?"

"Sorry, I won't be around to visit anymore."

"That's not what I meant."

"Well, you're right where you belong," he said, re-taping me. "Perhaps I am trying to drive you insane. Or at least make you look it, to discredit anything you might say. But maybe you're crazy already. Doesn't matter. You will be eventually. Your paperwork is being lost even as we speak."

SIXTY-FIVE

I had no idea what time it was. Night.

My breathing. A stringy, yellow spider on the ceiling. The taste of adhesive tape.

Needless to say, Quilp's visit had done little to improve my state of mind. I wondered what the electroshock might feel like. Maybe there's so much current, it knocks you out. Brain circuit overload, and after that, ignorance is bliss. And that was my optimistic scenario. I was also forced to consider a future wherein I would be unable to properly match subject and predicate, and drooling in the effort. Fortunately, I was in California and these handicaps might not disqualify me from finding employment as an astrologer or trance-channeler. Perhaps a position in rock 'n' roll.

Scuttling in the hallway. Closer now, and voices. And laughter. Christ. What was I, an amusing substitute for *The Late Late Show?* They were at the door. I strained around.

Spartacus. And Rudolph. And backing in slowly, with the practiced, fluid moves of the trained lawman, Sheriff Mike.

For one terrible instant I thought that in some wild cost-saving measure, or inbred vocational training program,

Barronville used patients as electroshock technicians, and the fate of my autonomic nervous system was in their not too steady hands.

But no. Rudolph came around to the foot of my gurney and began to push, Sheriff Mike steered in front, and we were out the door. As I thrashed about to learn what was happening, I caught glimpses of Spartacus running the point, darting ahead from corner to doorway, checking, waving if the coast was clear.

We accelerated, with me upside down and backwards, zinging through the corridors, racing, it appeared, back the same way I had come. Mike, in his excitement, had pulled the ranger hat down so tightly his ears bent out in pinched, pink right angles. Rudolph, pressing on, looking for all the world like an Olympian at the top of the bobsled run.

Down the long halls, faster and faster. To the flight deck? What was going on? The wheels bounced, the legs rocked, and I was on a lurching, jolting bed of jackhammering magic-fingers as we reached speeds far in excess of the manufacturer's most reckless estimates.

Faster still, Rudolph sometimes losing his footing as we fishtailed into the turns. The overhead lights strobed by, and the wind parted my hair.

But for us, the hospital was silent, seemingly deserted, and we probably would have completed our journey without hindrance had not my rescuers found it necessary to also bring along a small CD player on which the overture of *William Tell* now spun in digital audio splendor.

Spartacus rushed back, a blur of hand signals, my pals disappeared instantly, and I found myself bound, gagged, and rolling past the astonished face of attendant Scott like the credits to *The Lone Ranger.*

"What the fuck?"

He stopped me with a foot, suspended between fury and surprise. "What the fuck?"

And they were on him from behind. Stuffing a pillow-case over his head, they all practiced knockout karate chops on the back of his neck till somebody got it right. They tied him up, shoved him in a broom closet, and there was a slight delay while Rudolph read the labels on certain bottles and cans of cleaning fluid.

Off again. I realized I'd had my neck muscles cramped for some time, expecting at any moment to be smashed headfirst into who knows what unseen obstacle. Back up to speed. What were they doing? We hit the ramp, legs pumping, and came rolling out of the basement, the coast clear again. Zooming into the final straightaways, whipping through the curves, and back at the flight deck.

All the patients were in a group. A respectful but intense semicircle. And at their focus a voice I knew.

"So, gentlemen. There I was. The snakes behind me. A band of vicious Tsavi Indians charging out of the jungle and…" Spartacus, Rudolph, Sheriff Mike, and I came coasting in, "…ah, they're back. Good to see you, Dr. Brown." He peeled off my adhesive tape.

"Mr. Casbarian."

SIXTY-SIX

"At your service." He unsheathed his sword and made fast work of my restraining straps.

"What are you doing here?"

"Leaving. Quickly." He indicated a window where a small automobile jack had stretched the casing, freeing a half dozen bars in the process. And to my escape team, "You men will be all right?"

Spartacus raised his arm in salute. "Don't worry. I'll handle it."

"All right then. I thank you." He shook their hands.

I likewise, and suddenly, overcome, ventured, "Do you want to go with us?"

Mike and Spartacus put their hands to their mouths and blushed. Rudolph stared at his toes. "Oh, no, no, no."

"Why not?"

"You see," said Spartacus shyly, "we can't help it. We really are crazy."

"Sorry. I forgot."

"That's all right."

"Away," said Casbarian, and he was mobbed by back-slappers, hand shakers, and assisting arms, hoisting him to the window.

I was next, squeezing through, turning, waving at the last moment to acknowledge the applause. A twelve-foot drop. I pushed off into the night in what I assumed to be passable commando-style, and hit the ground running. The overall effect for which I was aiming was unfortunately spoiled because my ordeal on the gurney had worked loose the knots at my waist, and I was hard put to sprint and keep my pants from falling down at the same time. Casbarian whistled me to the wall.

"What's that?"

"Collapsible vaulting pole." He took a breath, rocked back on his heels, and was off, up, and over.

I retrieved the pole. In the old days, as participatory sports columnist, I'd spent a traumatic afternoon at Soldier Field in Chicago, working my way up to nine feet, six inches. This wall was no more than that, but the barbed wire on top added another foot and a half.

All right, and again, a situation with no options. I marked off my steps, took a breath, rocked back on my heels, and found myself in an insane asylum, running full speed toward a brick wall, in the dark, aiming a long pole at a shallow hole in the ground, with my pants falling down.

I made the plant, the laws of physics took over, and true to form I executed a respectable vault of approximately nine feet, six inches directly into the barbed wire.

Casbarian, however, had a thick blanket draped over the coils, and was waiting as well to break my fall as I disentangled myself and dropped over the side.

An astounding motorcycle was idling softly behind a pair of bushes by the side of the road. Candy-apple red with enormous winged fenders that curled over the top half of each wheel, an engine large enough to qualify for its own zip code, wide pleated seats, yards of art deco chrome gleaming even in the semidarkness, and a sidecar to match.

He swung into place, scanned the gauges. "All right. Let's go. Sorry it took me so long. Your computer entry was being deleted without explanation. Most difficult. And there was tampering in a cross-reference to a police report containing your very interesting statement about the murder of some dentist. Had to reconstruct the entire…"

"Mr. Casbarian, listen, there's someone else I believe is being held against her will. It's the daughter of the guy that had me thrown in here. I think they've got her in a cottage next to the…"

"You mean Qina is here?"

"What?"

"Best place for her, really."

"You know Qina?"

Mr. Casbarian put a hand on my shoulder. "I like you, son. You're not worth a jot as a psychologist, but I do like you." He then reached into the sidecar, pulled out a helmet sculpted much like the sweep of the fenders, and placed it over my head. "I know almost as much about Daniel Quilp as I do about myself. I've been after the swine for years. First got on to him when I was in Hollywood. He was running three major studios at once. In three separate disguises. I've been riding herd on you to keep tabs on Quilp."

"What are you talking about?"

"I was trying to get some sort of positive proof of a criminal act, but Quilp is a difficult man to get close to. So when his daughter went to a psychologist, I sensed a possible chink in the armor. Qina came to Dr. Fillmore, and I became a patient, too. When Fillmore's secretary told me she was transferred to you, I arranged to be transferred to you also."

"But..."

"Then Qina apparently disappeared, and at the same time you seemed to enter some sort of agreement with Quilp. Paying you to look for her was my guess. He wanted you around because he was curious what you might know about his wife's untimely death. But he underestimated you. Thought he could control you with money or some nonsense."

Mr. Casbarian motioned me to the sidecar. "Get in. Get in. There's an intravehicular communicator in our helmets."

A distant sizzle of static, but I could clearly hear him whistling between his teeth. I slid inside, my eyes level to an inscription on the gas tank.

"Sic itur ad astra."

Anticipatory roars of combustion. Casbarian flipped on a trio of fog lights, squared his shoulders, and ran up smoothly through the gears.

SIXTY-SEVEN

"So...you're not really crazy."

Casbarian laughed. "Certainly not."

"Well, Quilp is. He thinks he's the devil."

"Oh, but he is."

"Pardon me?"

"But I believe we can defeat him."

"We can?" I checked the speedometer. Eighty miles an hour.

"Yes. He appears to function like a mortal. I'm certain that in the past he's managed to save himself only by talking someone out of shooting or stabbing him, or sensing when it was coming from behind, or poison in a glass, a bomb under his chair. But times are more sophisticated, man, smarter. This may be our chance."

I see. Not crazy. And somehow, streaking through the night in my tiny capsule, I had allowed myself once again to be trapped by a loon. "Where are we going?"

"Ah, there's been an interesting new development."

"Oh, good."

"When I couldn't reach you by telephone, I thought I'd best check your apartment. You, of course, were absent, but I did find a police outline of a body and our mutual friend Rana Krishna peeking out a door. He had apparently been making popcorn nearby and emerged to see a man he described exactly as Daniel Quilp breaking somebody's neck. He'd been hiding behind a large-screen television in the MahaVala Diversion Sanctum down the hall."

"Rana Krishna? Why didn't he tell the police?"

"Distancing himself from the world of sensation. But as you remember, I had as much as saved his bacon the other night, and he was quite anxious to share this hazardous secret with someone he trusted."

"I'll strangle him."

"He was quite rattled. I phoned Dr. Fillmore and convinced him to come babysit. Now, with Rana Krishna as eyewitness and you supplying the motive, all we have to do is phone Lieutenant Scharfman first thing in the morning and pick Quilp up."

"Quilp's leaving tonight."

"What?"

"That's what he told me. Things are getting too hot for him and he's packing it in tonight."

"Good God."

SIXTY-EIGHT

We have, all of us, had moments like this. Possibly with a New York cab driver, possibly a friend who has had too much to drink or is attempting to show off. You find yourself a passenger in a vehicle going much too fast, and because the distance to be covered is short, the social circumstances uncomfortable, or because you feel any attempt to change the situation for the better can only make it worse, you do nothing.

But even those who have experienced these anxious moments fingering the seat belt, measuring each breath, pressing a nonexistent brake into the floor mat, cannot possibly begin to understand the sheer, powerless, unprotected terror of 120 miles an hour in a sidecar.

I had always thought the last place in the world I wanted to be was on the back of a motorcycle, but when Casbarian cranked us into triple figures and I was thrown to the rear of my fragile shell, I knew I'd been wrong. Time compressed, speed became something almost tangible, the world rushed at me in ways my senses could not fully absorb.

"Brown…Brown!"

"What?"

"Call Lieutenant Scharfman."

"What?"

"There's a phone in the console. Have him meet us at Quilp's."

"I can't call Lieutenant Scharfman. He thinks I'm insane."

"Ha. Right. Call Dr. Fillmore. Scharfman will want Rana Krishna along anyway to make a positive ID."

"Fillmore."

"Right. Have him get everyone to Quilp's, but they are to wait for us at the foot of the drive."

"OK. OK. I'll call Fillmore. Where is he?"

"Your apartment."

"My apartment? How did they get in there?"

"As your landlord, Rana Krishna had the keys with him. It was the most convenient."

"It was, huh? Oh, all right."

But in order to use the phone, it was necessary to take off my helmet. The backwash immediately whipped my hair into my eyes. G-forces widened my cheeks, great, chunky insects thwacked off my teeth.

A female voice. "Brown residence."

"Who is this?"

"Who's this?"

"This is Brown. You're on my telephone."

"Brown! It's me. Rebecca."

"Rebecca? What are you doing in my apartment?"

"I'm in town for the motorcycle races. Stopped by to see it you wanted to tag along."

"Rebecca...is there a fat guy there? And a little jerk wearing robes?"

"Brown, you're not going to believe this, but that's Joel."

"Who?"

"My brother, Joel. With the robes."

"Rana Krishna is your brother?"

"Isn't it too much? We knew he was in California, but nobody in the family had heard from him in years. Hold on. He wants to talk."

Rana Krishna, Rebecca Siegelman's brother. Was I to be plagued by this family the rest of my life? Was I some special project of theirs, singled out for torment?

"Brown?"

"Hi, Joel."

"Shut up with that. Where are you?"

I saw where I was, passing a gasoline truck.

"Never mind. Put Fillmore on."

"What's supposed to happen to me?"

"Nothing. You're a witness. You've got to identity that guy, that's all."

"You know him, right? What a fuckin' monster. Snapped his neck in half a second. Made a sort of crackling sound. Worse than you can ever imagine. Grabbed the old guy like he was a chicken. Shoved his chin against..."

"All right! Just calm down. Give the phone to Fillmore."

"Yeah...OK. He's right here."

"Brown? Where you been, man?"

I ran things down for Fillmore. He was unenthusiastic, to be sure, but finally agreed to find Lieutenant Scharfman and get the whole entourage out to Quilp's as quickly as possible. The last thing I heard before he clicked off was the high-pitched, implacable voice of Rebecca, bleating excitedly in the background.

"I call driver! I get to be driver!"

SIXTY-NINE

I cradled the phone, re-helmeted. Mr. Casbarian and I exchanged nods, and he shifted into what must have been seventh gear. We came off the crest of a hill. A yapping dog, miscalculating our speed, claiming our lane. Casbarian twitched the handlebars, and I felt the wheels beneath me leave the ground. The beginning of a spin as we exceeded the coefficient of sliding friction. Oncoming traffic blurred, the rear tire caught and jerked, my head slammed into the sidewall, flicks of trees, and we were off the road in a cloud of dust.

Gravel shots to my throat, a bounce, and back on the highway. I pressed the heels of my hands into my thighs, took a deep breath, and adopted the dulcet, persuasive tones that, I thought, I'd used on him so successfully in the past.

"Mr. Casbarian. Wonderful machine. Ahh, just amazing. Can I give it a try?"

He laughed good-naturedly. "I think I better take it in, Brown. You sit back and enjoy yourself."

SEVENTY

We were the last to arrive. Lieutenant Scharfman had his notebook out and was frowning at Rana Krishna. Fillmore straddled a fender of the Austin Healey, fingering a bagel. And Rebecca ran up to meet us.

In her red jumpsuit, she looked like she was modeling leisurewear for Santa Claus, but I did notice the beginning of a waist.

"Brown! Isn't this exciting? A murder investigation."

I uncoiled myself from the sidecar. During the course of our ride, I'd had ample time to tighten and retighten the knots in the waist of my pants, but seemed to have lost a sandal somewhere. Lieutenant Scharfman raised an eyebrow in my direction, turned questioningly to Fillmore.

Rebecca giggled. "Nice threads. By the way, your carburetors need adjusting."

Casbarian and Lieutenant Scharfman found each other, and the rest of us paired off as well, I, dragging Fillmore to one side; and, summarily rejected, Rebecca returning to Rana Krishna to discuss old times.

"Jesus Christ, man. What are you, a refugee from the clown school infirmary?"

"Fillmore…all these people are nuts."

"I know. Let's get breakfast."

"I'm not going anywhere dressed like this."

"We'll do takeout."

"What's open?"

"There's that place across from the bus depot."

"Oh, all right. Who's got my keys?"

Rebecca. In the driver's seat. Rana Krishna alongside. "Brown. Come on."

Casbarian had parked his bike just off the road. "Brown, hurry," he urged, getting into the Scharfmanmobile.

I took Fillmore's bagel. "Let's get this over with."

"Give that back. OK. You're buying breakfast, man."

I held out my nonexistent pockets. "With what, Fillmore?"

"Get in." An order from the lieutenant.

I slid in behind Casbarian. Fillmore slid in beside me. Rebecca, rebuffed, laid rubber, passing us before Scharfman had shifted into drive.

She had pulled up next to the house and was leaning back in her seat, arms folded, while Scharfman parked at a discreet distance. I noticed a fresh dent in my rear right quarter panel.

These were the first minutes of morning; the tops of trees began to emerge from the horizon. Scharfman pretended to study the quiet pockets of shadows ringing the house, but Casbarian had already taken a few tentative steps, and he hustled to catch up.

I saw no reason to move. Nor, apparently, did Fillmore, and we sat there, leisurely passing the bagel back and forth, chewing in meditative silence. Rebecca was out of the

Healey now, waiting for Casbarian and the lieutenant. Rana Krishna opted for a change in position and was sort of side-stepping watchfully back in our direction.

And then I noticed the silhouette of a monkey, hanging from one of the upstairs gutters. It seemed that I ought to get confirmation of this from Fillmore. I turned, he was picking crumbs off his lap, and in the window behind, the coil of a stupendous, muscular snake looped in lazy descent.

Unable to move, I watched a milky, muddy drop of morning dew zigzag slowly along its scales. A head peeked in, the forked threads of its tongue testing the air.

"Ya." I reached for my door handle, but became disinclined to actually use it when I saw the lion. Then a zebra charged by, and a few seconds later from the opposite direction, something large with horns.

Mr. Casbarian. "Run!"

Everybody seemed to but us. As I thought I had by far the safest seat, however, I assumed this advice did not apply to me.

"Run! Get out of the car!"

An edge of genuine, frenzied appeal that time. Fillmore went rigid and then, certainly oblivious to the smorgasbord of zoological terrors raging without, pushed through his door, snake and all.

"Brown! Move it! Now!"

It was only from the deepest reaches of my soul, in that truest sense of myself that knew I had never once been wronged, but, in fact, frequently and repeatedly saved by Mr. Casbarian, that orders were issued to the necessary muscles to move me out of that car. And once out, once I actually saw the rhinoceros and the bears, I had no difficulty supplying the necessary acceleration.

"The other way! The other way!"

Because Quilp was on his front steps, holding what could only have been one of those missile launchers, and I was moving right toward him. He was smiling, appearing to enjoy his moment, but somehow what was most disturbing was that his hair was messed up, a thing that had not previously seemed possible. There were long, thick stains on his jacket where grease had oozed from a joint of the trigger controls, and one of his legs began to twitch about, as though he were warming up for an Appalachian folk dance.

"I order you to drop that," said Lieutenant Scharfman in a voice that held no hope of being obeyed. In fairness, it must be said that had the lieutenant not been in full gallop himself at the time, he might have found the courage to squeeze off a shot.

Quilp, however, fired first.

SEVENTY-ONE

Beyond what I considered noise, more a concussion. A thunderous shock of sound that, while it lived, was master of everything. I was thrown to the ground, but not until the force of the blast had lifted my legs over my head and flung me horizontally at a speed that kept me airborne long enough to think about it.

Lieutenant Scharfman's car was gone. In its place, a towering, orange fireball nestled perfectly in its own crater. The energy, so intense a mini-climate was created to accommodate the tear in the elements. Everything around suddenly pushed by winds, singed, instantly scorched by the heat. The silver-blue cap of morning filled with flying leaves and branches, eddies of smoke, falling redwoods, an unbroken shower of dirt.

"Brown? Brown! Where are you?"

This was Rebecca, so I kept quiet.

"Brown?"

Last to react, I had gotten much the worst of it. Of my shirt, only the collar and one sleeve remained. My pants were torn at the knees and shredded beneath that.

"There you are."

I still had half a bagel, threw it at a dazed panther. Rebecca came up under my shoulder, helped me to my feet. We limped to Rana Krishna, sitting against a tree stump with most of a dead alligator in his lap (though it could have been a crocodile).

She bent over, smacked him on the cheek. "Snap out of it." Again. "Get up." We did it for him, each on an arm.

Fillmore and the lieutenant had reassembled at the Healey, blackened and scarred now, but spared the direct vectors of the explosion. Fillmore was muddy, bleeding from the nose, and Lieutenant Scharfman looked like he had taken a demonstration ride in the electric chair, but I could see that he'd crossed the line from fear to anger. Something in the moment had found its way into his cerebral cortex and pushed the button labeled John Wayne.

Flashing between the trees, Quilp in a black convertible, speeding around the outer drive.

Scharfman growled, "Let's get the son of a bitch."

Rebecca already had the Healey rolling, and we jumped in. A tight fit, but someone was missing. "Where's Mr. Casbarian?"

Fillmore. "I saw him running away."

"Me too," said Rebecca, shouting now as my engine was revved into unexplored territory.

Mr. Casbarian, a coward? If such a thing could happen, what hope was there for a guy like me?

The two driveways converged; we came through the gates right on Quilp's bumper. "Nobody blows up my car and gets away with it!" screamed the lieutenant predictably.

And as we sped onto the road, past Casbarian's motorcycle parked to one side, a glimpse of him crouched behind. Hiding?

In and out of Mill Valley, the streets narrow and Rebecca holding her own. Racing toward the freeway, Quilp stretching a lead on the straightaways, but the Healey gaining it back in the curves.

Fillmore and I, having instantly conspired to sandwich Rana Krishna on the petite rear jump seat, now squashed him even more as we fought to stay aboard.

And we hit the 101, swerving down the entry ramp, heading south. Hours before the morning rush, a few oversize trucks, a sprinkling of cars. We wove a path through. Quilp bouncing into guardrails, spinning off a hubcap, Rebecca bearing down on the accelerator, and Rana Krishna, "You're breaking my leg!"

We roared up over Sausalito, our extra poundage penalizing us on the ascent. Down through the tunnel, Quilp comfortably in front now, heading onto the Golden Gate.

A shimmering blur, a red one, loud, passing us, flying onto the bridge. Mr. Casbarian, minus the sidecar, in hot pursuit. I found myself cheering.

Across and into the city, traffic knotting up, Quilp violating all rules not only for automobiles, but pedestrians as well. Over the curb onto manicured lawns, through parking lots, down heavily filled sidewalks. Scharfman shouting, Fillmore shouting, though for different reasons. A recent turn had left him sprawled over the trunk, hanging on with a pudgy ankle wedged under the seat. I caught his necktie flapping in the wind and pulled him up.

Back onto the freeway a distant third, with the law-abiding Mr. Casbarian also having given up ground. Five lanes here and pretty straight, both working to our disadvantage. Quilp's taillights shrinking out of sight and more cars, obstructing our view. We pressed on, Rebecca completely absorbed in her task, bent over the steering wheel, squeezing it to force out any extra horsepower.

It was the airport. We had lost Quilp, but in the distance, Casbarian's bike, making the turn, disappearing behind a banked overpass.

"Yaah!" A groan of primeval frustration from the lieutenant. He laid his hand on the horn, screaming, waving his badge furiously at startled motorists as we struggled to stay in the chase.

Rebecca squealing onto the airport turnoff and across the tangle of arrival, departure, rental cars only, buses, garage lanes, without touching the brake. We made a complete circuit, defeated, and had begun a pass along the service road when I caught sight of the motorcycle, tipped over on a runway.

"The private terminal. There! Make a right."

Scharfman pushed his way through the miniature lobby, shoving his credentials at a sleepy, suddenly panicked janitor, and we ran, limped, and shouted onto the tarmac.

The sun had burned off all but the highest layers of morning dusk. A rumble, splitting into a roar as a small jet lifted overhead. Ice blue behind a hooked silver nose. It kicked into a stiff vertical climb trailing soft plumes beneath.

Hot winds sent tremors into the observation windows, pushed us back, and fluttered what was left of my clothing.

Scharfman collared a doughnut-eating fellow in coveralls. "Who's on that plane?"

"I dunno. Some guy. Maybe two."

Banking slightly east over the bay, its sharp contours showing black against the rising sun. Streaking for outer space, but canting gradually, uncomfortably, appearing to lead with its tail, overturning just below the clouds, backward. It hung there a while, noiseless, floating, unnaturally twisting to one side, and began to fall. Then plummeting, spinning savagely, nose first, screaming back to earth.

We tracked the descent in a state of petrified fascination, but I finally needed to turn away and noticed a small pip, ejected, dropping in a tiny, separate arc. The thing seemed to lurch, changing trajectory. I thought it was a man, though I couldn't be sure as the sun was in my eyes, and as I followed him down, I saw a pair of extra limbs sprouting from his back. He swooped lower, unfurling cadaverous, webbed wings of Mesozoic dimension, and slowly flapped off.

And Quilp's jet, plunging for Candlestick Park, San Francisco Bay holding, reverberating the howl.

I realized that for some time I had been gnawing a large hole into the first joint of my index finger and was reflexively chewing the missing patch to pulp. I looked down at the raw flesh, a white strip of bone, as the crush spread back across my tongue.

EPILOGUE

I am with Casbarian. I am, in fact, Casbarian's sidekick. We are in Tangier, on the trail of Daniel Quilp. Evidence against him keeps mounting irrefutably. We now know he was also Bernice Glotsky in Miami, Harry Lime in Vienna, Dr. Bullfinch in Cape Town, and in the Orient, Feotan Nonato.

After Mr. Casbarian (third place in SportJet/Super Stock, Reno Air Races, 1991) pulled Quilp's plane out of the dive in the nick of time, I had two offers—one of marriage, from Rebecca, and one of exotic food, expensive women, high-performance cars, and international high life, from Casbarian. I chose the second, and the promised enticements are indeed at hand.

As I write this we are in the bar of the Hotel Phoenicia, Casbarian with the owner, the entrancing Madame Carol demonstrating the correct way to make a Morning After (1 egg white, 1 teaspoon anisette syrup, 1 glass absinthe, stir briskly, dash of soda on top). There was a friend for me, and in truth, with the proper orthodontia she would have been fine, but things just didn't work out. To be fair though, I haven't been myself since the incident at the airport.

One can't really see much looking into the sun, and as all other eyes were on the falling plane, and as I still wore the uniform of a lunatic, the issue was never pressed. But neither was it internally resolved.

For purposes of his report, Lieutenant Scharfman claimed to have seen a large splash, but, of course, no body has been found. Nor any trace of Ann Adrian or the mysterious Dr. Einstein.

But Scharfman did give me back my check, and I still have it, framed, on the wall over Fillmore's desk at Stanford. The lawyers tell me it will take a while, years, until Quilp's affairs can be untangled, but as a legitimate creditor I, we, will one day collect.

There was a sufficient amount allocated to keep Qina in Barronville for the rest of her life, and with the help of Dr. Limbus-Edgington, that's probably how much time she'll need. I went to visit her once, but she took me for the maid and I spent an afternoon cleaning out her cottage. The old gang was glad to see me, however, and let me know the position at second base was only temporarily filled pending my possible return.

Rebecca, a practical woman with a great job, punched me an affectionate farewell in the shoulder and went home to stalk a Pulitzer Prize. Rana Krishna held out as long as he could, but when a group of visiting Rosicrucians claimed to hear voices laughing and calling for "Dr. Brown" in the hallways of the MahaVala Building, he packed for the East Coast. He is now selling a Junior Miss line for his father's dress company and is largely responsible for the recent robe craze sweeping fashion-conscious teenagers in New England.

Fillmore bought me a send-off breakfast, and we said good-bye in the parking lot of Sam's Anchor Café. He was holding a stack of papers, the dream journals of an elderly lady whose therapy was proving a delight. We had been discussing my hallucination. According to Fillmore, after rationality killed God, modern man started thrashing about for new myths to nurture his soul. Some turned to Marx, a later generation to Freud, then science, and now it was a need to believe in benign, super-intelligent creatures from outer space.

"And in your case, old pal..." he began, smiling. But a strong, unexpected gust of wind came up off the water. The last I saw of Fillmore, he was running down the street, gathering an old woman's dreams in his arms.

ABOUT THE AUTHOR

 James Polster is a movie pro-
ducer, novelist, and journalist
who earned graduate degrees
from Harvard University and
Columbia University. A National
Fellow of the Explorers Club, he
has traveled the world profiling
international luminaries such as
Indira Gandhi and Donald Trump and covering such major
athletic events as the Duran/Leonard Superfight and the
World Championships of Elephant Polo. His award-winning
first book, *A Guest in the Jungle*, helped focus a spotlight on
the disappearing Amazon rain forest, and his second book,
Brown, was named by *Publishers Weekly* as a Best Book of the
Year. For his third book, *The Graduate Student*, Polster drew
on his experiences working at Columbia Pictures and NBC.